PERVATORY

PERVATORY

RM VAUGHAN

Coach House Books | Toronto

first edition

Published with the generous assistance of the Canada Council for the Arts and the Ontario Arts Council. Coach House Books also acknowledges the support of the Government of Canada through the Canada Book Fund.

LIBRARY AND ARCHIVES CANADA CATALOGUING IN PUBLICATION

Title: Pervatory / RM Vaughan.
Names: Vaughan, R. M. (Richard Murray), 1965-2020, author.
Identifiers: Canadiana (print) 20210394080 | Canadiana (ebook) 20210394102 | ISBN 9781552454374 (softcover) | ISBN 9781770567054 (PDF) | ISBN 9781770567047 (EPUB)
Classification: LCC PS8593.A94 P47 2023 | DDC C13/.54—dc23

Pervatory is available as an ebook: ISBN 978 1 77056 704 7 (EPUB), ISBN 978 1 77056 705 4 (PDF)

Purchase of the print version of this book entitles you to a free digital copy. To claim your ebook of this title, please email sales@chbooks.com with proof of purchase. (Coach House Books reserves the right to terminate the free digital download offer at any time.)

' … and the Devil, though he may purchase, does not keep faith.'

– Bram Stoker

'on the wall that separates
our wakefulness from a dream
a mirror hangs'

– Jānis Rokpelnis

I know what it means to be sane.

I know what it means to read the world as the world, as itself. I know what it means to tell possible from impossible, static from fantastic, real from false. I know what it means to walk into a room, any room, and say to myself: here are the chairs, here are some flowers, here is a glass of water, here are my shoes. Here I am at peace. I know the difference between a situation and a manifestation. I know my own self, and I know others. Isn't that enough?

A year ago, if you had told me that I would be kept, now, in this resting place, tucked under a blanket, smothered by quiet, eating bland food and drinking only milky tea, a man not so much resigned to his situation as unable to think of – indeed actively stopped from thinking of – another previous, fuller life, I would have said you were mad.

Now, it's me who is mad. Or so I am told in the politest possible but inescapably conclusive fashion. The insane are permitted little (if they are caught, that is), and I am allowed almost nothing. Therefore, I must be insane. I got caught.

I can write, but I can't send letters. I can listen to music, but it must be simple and clear, childish. Mozart is permitted, Bach is not. Repetitive dance music is tolerated, but songs with lyrics are screened. And always rejected. Television is entirely forbidden. You see, I am so easily set off.

A year ago, I left my home. I was middle-aged, bored, unhealthy, stuck in my habits, and loveless. Perfectly normal, in other words. Hatefully normal. At least that's cured. I hated myself and wanted an adventure. I got what I wanted. I cannot expect to be forgiven.

Although I am never outside this room, or, to be fair, so rarely outside this room I am beginning to forget life's eternal things, such as the feel of a cold wind, how grass smells when it is wet, the magic of the moon, I have, I would argue perversely, a pair of shoes. White canvas shoes, with flat soles and rubber lining (but, of course, no shoelaces); simple six-hole lace-up runners. The hospital probably buys them in bulk. The shoes smell of off-gassing plastic, as does the cutlery.

When my keepers removed the shoelaces, they left the eyelets intact – twenty-four little circles of tin, so easy to remove. I've taken off two so far. Nobody notices. Pinched into a half-circle then pinched again into a crude triangle, the tin circles make a simple carving tool, a tiny trawl small as a needle.

With my little cutter, I scratch words onto my walls, in a script smaller and thinner than the legs of an ant. (I know because I have checked. Despite the hospital's every precaution, the daily sweeping I am tasked with, and the weekly bleaching the orderlies perform with resentful gusto, their mops slapping the tiles so sharply it makes me jump, my room is still visited by black ants no bigger than an eyelash.)

I am fond of busy and small creatures. I delight in anything hapless but occupied, in any animal with its own agenda.

With my tin triangle I scratch words and pictures, hints and traces. So far, no one has noticed my decorations. I still have some art in me yet.

Here is what I have etched into the wall beside my bed, words and pictures:

Abraham and Isaac.

Manfred, Paul, Udo, Pieter, Walter, Basil … (The list grows daily, it's a slow process, all this remembering.)

Alexandar. Alexandar. Alexandar.

The Six of Wands. The Prince of Cups.

A drawing of a lit candle. A drawing of a knife. A drawing of three hand bells. A drawing of a closed eye, inside a diamond shape, inside an imperfect circle.

A curling trail of ivy, vines, and leaves (I hope to reach the ceiling someday).

An unbroken line running directly above where I rest my head at night. The line is the exact same length as my pillow. I align my pillow and the trace before I sleep.

An old-fashioned train lantern with a circular handle and a wick. For rays of light, I scratched off fingernail-sized strips of paint. Under the buttery white paint, I discovered, the walls are slate black, glossy. I wish I had not done this one. It will be the first thing they notice, whenever they care to notice.

My name: Martin Murray Heather. A name fit for a weakling. Life is not entirely unjust.

Berlin is lousy with children. It's the first thing visitors notice. Wobbling, pin-legged children. Children with blanched hair, uniformly off-white in colour, hair thin as thread and unspooling in all directions.

All the children's impulses are met and satisfied. Everything is for 'das kinder' – kinder parks where no dog, bottle, cigarette, stray adults, nor layabouts may enter. Do not wander in to admire the flowers unless you have a child under your arm.

In Berlin, children play in traffic. They run entire blocks, knees knocking, away, away, free from their parents, run distances from their strollers that would make a parent in Canada scream in terror. Entire blocks. They run toward the cars, toward the curb, daring death and howling at danger. Berlin children know instinctively that the short-pants years are their time and the city is their place, road rules be damned. Gravity be damned. At first, it's disconcerting. You think: *Catch that kid!* But you stop, because no one else is thinking the same.

Let them run, bellowing their chipmunk yips to the traffic. Their minders merely shrug, if they notice at all. I have only seen one child be scolded, and in English. Tourists, I guess. Like me.

Kinder-clothing kiosks sell capes and leggings printed with red-capped mushrooms, four-leaf clovers, grinning bats, and, of course, Berlin's mascot bears. Blue bears, green bears, pink and purple bears – anything but brown or black bears. That would be too real.

There is plenty of time for the cruel realities of nature later, the parents nod.

Can it be healthy, living in a babied world? Healthy for us – us adults, I mean – people with schedules and tasks? Or at least the pretense of things to do?

When I arrived at my furnished rental, I looked at all the gaudy, candy-coloured IKEA trappings – tomato-red chairs, pumpkin and tangerine drapes, the dozens of pink pillows I had to, for my sanity (or snobbery, call it either), put into the closet along with the printed paper lanterns) – and it occurred to me that the person who decorated this bonbonerie, a Parisian named Madame Millard, truly hates adult life. She wants to be a child again.

Madame Millard is my landlady, but I've never laid eyes on her. We communicate only via email. A Parisian who never sets foot in Berlin, she rents out her 'second home,' as do all middle-class Berliners, for easy money. She decorated the flat like a nursery; in that way, at least, she is a Berliner. I imagine Madame Millard in blue clogs, lime-green leggings, and a cotton dress decorated with felt daisies. I imagine a girl-woman. The armoire in the bedroom is stuffed with empty vintage hat boxes tied with lavender ribbons.

Every morning there's a belch of the water pipes, the fucking pipes. Europe is old, and so are its pipes – I knew what I was getting into. Water does not move through pipes at Willibald-Alexis-Strasse 55 – it charges, angry as a riptide. Turn on the tap to rinse off your hands and eleven different pipes in three places, bedroom to front door, chug and retch like you're hurting the building. The roar, especially in the middle of the night, unsettles me, makes me feel like an intruder. And I do not sleep soundly, never have.

Sometimes the pipes tap out a muffled undersound, a tinkle beneath the crash, like the sound of a silver ring hitting the basin of a sink. The sound comes and goes, inconsistent and accidental.

I imagine a diamond or a lost coin making its way around and around the building's water circuit, perhaps since before I was born.

And, of course, I think of all the things I've thrown away in a panic, the gems and the coins and the good friends.

Me and Berlin. A love story.

I don't think I really looked at the city the first couple of weeks I was here. All I did was run from museum to leather bar to museum. But now that I'm settled I have to be more patient, have to wait in line to buy milk and bread and matches and light bulbs like everybody else, have to bump up against Germans who are also not on frantic sexual or High Art agendas. Germans and Turks, I should say – people with jobs, people who save and return their beer bottles, feed their kids Nutella on toast every morning, and worry about their savings. The feeling of the city is very different than what I expected, especially in one keen way: I see now that Berlin is not a glamorous place.

German glamour is cheap, grubby, and smells a bit of lard and worn shoes. To be glamorous in Germany is to be conspicuously languid, half-awake, like a hippie. Oh, everyone tries. There are plenty of places to try: microbars with specialty music, noisy Italian cafés, the relic bars, left over from or manufactured in imitation of the glorious 1920s, a time never far from Berliners' minds. The whole Sally Bowles number, in tights and bowlers. But for true glamour, you need stakes, and the stakes in Berlin are simply not high. There is no urgency to life in Berlin, only the maintenance of pleasure. So Berlin is a perfect city for mid-life, the resignation years.

Berliners don't suffer from status anxiety. Going to an art opening is no more fancy or socially ambitious than sipping a beer at your corner bierhaus or going shopping for beets and carrots. And a celebrity in Germany is really only a celebrity when she comes from the United States or England. There are no stakes to fret over. A party is a night at home. You can take the dog to the park or take yourself around the corner and bend over a fisting bench in a filthy piss-stained backroom. It's all the same. Nothing seems to register with Berliners as exciting or novel or extreme.

I find this refusal to make anything too important refreshing after Toronto, the city that won't let itself sleep. Berliners are not blasé and are never bored; they are just used to having everything at once, for centuries.

For instance, until I came here, I'd never met people more concerned with creating, without ever showing their concern, the exact and correct atmosphere for casual sex. Maybe that's why I feel so much freer here. Too free, my Canadian mind tells me. I have nothing to prove, I'm nameless. I fuck, I write, I wander. I've lost my footing.

No. I've lost nothing. I threw it away. Because in Berlin, so very little counts. In Toronto, whatever I do counts too much.

Once I hid all the landlady's junk art and pastel pillows, I was happy to find that my sublet apartment was actually quite cute, airy, and bright. It's the kind of place you feel justified buying expensive flowers for, an apartment that just needs a couple of bottles of eight-euro wine and a table crammed with scented twinkling candles to feel special. An apartment for a Writer. God help me.

From the boxy and spare wooden chairs to the bleached barnboard floors to the five-foot-tall windows to the deep, drowning-deep, tub, the silver sheer curtains, and the long, overstuffed daybed, the apartment declared itself a Writer's Study. I never found out who the previous subletter was, but I was certain she (I thought 'she,' always, and strongly so) didn't work for the civic government, or Deutsche Bank, or some international food-relief agency. Nobody could live between those walls and wake up every morning, pull back the carrot-coloured swag curtains, feel the early sun on her face, and then methodically iron a skirt, polish her shoes, set up meetings by text message, read files and reports. She would have to write a poem and do no more.

I lived a few blocks north of the old Tempelhof Airport, a massive inner-city airport abandoned in 2008 and turned into a nature preserve and leisure park; an airport built, Germans like to tell each other, on Knights Templar land. Such busy little plotters, those Templars. Could they have imagined that one day their secret forest would be a ghost port, that terriers and beagles would skitter and yip through the same chestnut orchards where wild boars used to kill peasants, that in-line skating would replace blood sacrifices, pop music prayers, that flat stones would hold picnic lunches wrapped in wax paper, not severed heads swaddled in burlap?

One afternoon, I noticed a series of large black signs running along the northern edge of the park, billboard-sized squares posted low to the ground and covered in bold, all-caps white text, English text. Obviously, it was an art project. The text was all about Victor Hugo and his supposed dream of a united Europe. This was news to me. I thought Hugo hated the English, for starters. Anyway, the project was ruefully optimistic. Wounds and healing and voices raised in harmony, that sort of thing.

I read it all. I had nothing else to do in the late afternoons.

Some clever marketer had paired every one of the art billboards with a frantic, lurid poster for a visiting circus. They still have circuses in Berlin, the old-fashioned kind, with animals (zebras on the poster, likely painted horses – it can't be legal to ride zebras, not even in Berlin) and mustachioed men in Tarzan kilts lifting blond girls on cows, leering clowns in pointy dunce caps, and swarthy fellows in tails cracking riding whips.

The clown at the centre of the poster had enormous pointed ears. So, I remembered reading once, did Victor Hugo. Great flapping saucepans on the sides of his head. How writerly of me to make the connection. Yes, I disgust myself.

Searching the cupboards for a rag to wipe coffee grounds out of the kitchen sink, I found eleven tins and three plastic tubs, all unopened and all marked in what I assumed to be Russian. I guessed they were left behind by the previous tenant, the mystery lady (who may have been a man, but I doubt it).

I opened one tin and one tub. The tin contained a rust-red powder, which I took to be paprika, but it had no smell, and I was not about to taste it – what if, I thought, it's lye or some Russian version of hair dye?

The plastic tub was bursting with a thick yellow concoction that looked like mustard. The goo had congealed on the top and was covered by a dry, hard skin, a taut, pebbled skin with deep brown seams, seams that branched out across the tight surface and up onto the inside walls of the tub like roots, like dried veins.

Floor wax, I told myself, it's floor wax. Close the lid and carry on. Put everything back where you found it. This is not your home.

That night, I read the Tarot. I do most nights.

The spread was simple, a three-card quickie: Six of Wands, Five of Pentacles, Justice.

Tribulation, a five in a five or perfect imperfection, equanimity. A stumblebum forecast.

I would read the Tarot now if I was permitted, allowed my magics. I miss it.

Berlin is a haunted city. As well it should be. But so far I've heard only one Nazi joke, and the word *Nazi* was not used. It came out so naturally.

I was talking to a chunky, smiling, very tanned guy in Quälgeist, the rough gay sex club on Mehringdamm, a black, cum-encrusted hole just seven minutes from my innocent, cookies-and-milk, naptime-and-counting-books building. Really, all I wanted was a good fucking, but he had the Canada Question, the one about Quebec, and I gave him the Canada Answer, the one about multiculturalism, and off he went, into a shrugging monologue about the Bad Time Germans Don't Name.

Honestly, the subject was the last thing I want to talk about to a German, any German, but I was glad to get it out of the way in my first week. It's almost like Germans can tell if the new guy hasn't yet had the Bad Time conversation (which is not a conversation, but more of a nod, a goofed apology). Well, here goes … and then, having done the Bad Time job, the German goes back to drinking and smoking, to cocks and tongues and real things.

The Bad Time is not real to Germans anymore. Only the language around the Bad Time has any power now, and every sentence ends with a resigned half chuckle. I don't know how one can own that history, and I don't want to learn. I'm glad to be done with the whole stupid dance, the pretty footwork, the drunken walk on uneven cobbles. It's not my business.

The dream begins with a dog and a river. Later, a pocket is opened – a back pocket on a pair of trousers, a breast pocket in a long coat, a secret compartment inside a shoulder bag, sealed with a zipper. In one version, a hole in the ground, a cavity, no bigger than a billiard table corner net.

The dog bumbles along before me, looking back every few feet, checking – Are you still there? Do you still love me? Are we on the path together? – as dogs will, ever in the present tense. If there is snow beneath our feet, the dog carefully breaks a path for me, because I am barefoot, dead from the knees down. If there is grass and sunshine, the dog darts ahead, then slows, winks, and sniffs, arrowing his nose at crickets, fat bees, any pile of filth. So far, the dog has been black, and carroty red, and long-haired and short-haired. But he (it is always a he) remains the same size and type: a retriever, crossed with a hound. A dog bred for the charm of his lopsided gait. He is clumsy and perfectly adept, as dogs will be. He is never white, but his muzzle is greying. And I adore him.

The problem is the river. I cannot see the whole of it, only the piddling runoffs that leak over the banks. A river is meant to line the land, mark and break space, interrupt the dull earth. The dog knows his way because he can smell the width and depth of the river, knows it instantly, can feel inside his nostrils the patches of sunlight that warm the surface, bringing tiny organisms to the surface to feed, tiny fetid organisms, creatures that live on waste and green algae and each other, treats he would like to taste. But I am lost.

The dream progresses at a different pace in each version – a matter of seconds pass or an entire afternoon. There is a frustrating limitlessness to the process, because I know, from the start, how events will conclude, and I am anxious to get to the sweet part, the reveal.

The dog halts, sits, opens his mouth, and makes a sound like a gear jammed up, a gear perhaps clogged with wads of tinfoil, something crinkly, a sound like a tired hinge – a simple, violent sound you could hear on any street corner, from any fussy car or crusted shutter. Not a dog sound. Not an animal sound at all, but oddly comforting in its own odd way, like the grinding pop of a toaster, the familiar click of a bedroom light switch, a pendant circling a silver chain.

And that's my cue, the metallic bark. The dog stares forward and I search, search for the pocket. It can be anywhere, but it is usually inside my coat. So far, there have been nine dreams, and in six of them, the pocket, the helpful pocket, has been right to hand, close to my chest. I burrow in, fingers tingling. The dog has moved away. I hear splashing, paws slapping water, panting, but I can't see him anymore. He hardly matters. My hand is hot. I am greedy and childish, smaller now. I hardly matter.

Only, what is inside? What is inside? What is inside the pocket?

The U-Bahn was a furnace. By the fourth step down to the tracks, my back was always slick, late summer or midwinter. I'd take off my leather jacket and sling it over my right forearm, where it stuck, making a red mark.

The heat was dry but not still. Particles wafted all around, flecks of axle grease caked with dust, cigarette ash, doughnut crumbs, other skins. No matter the time of day, the station, Platz der Luftbrücke, my local, was nearly empty. There were no senior citizens, no teens – the most reliable users of tunnels and trains. Once, I saw a businessman. His face was red and angry, as if he'd been robbed of his wallet, or, more likely, his car was stalled. His suit was beautiful, fog grey with the thinnest chalk stripe, topped off with a sapphire tie. His jaw was strong but fixed, rage set, flattening his lips. He had never been in a place so dirty in all his life.

Every Wednesday at 5:00 p.m. and Saturday at 9:00 p.m., I rode the U6 from Platz der Luftbrücke to Tempelhof. From Tempelhof, I rode the S-Bahn to Innsbrucker Platz. Then I walked. No, hurried. Rushed up Haupstrasse to Sachsendamm, to the Böse Buben, number 77 Sachsendamm … only to stand about for an hour, another hour, stand about again, in this simple place, two floors of red rooms with black furniture, only the latest dark, too-warm bar to over-occupy my mind. The Black Eagle in Toronto. The Hole in the Wall Saloon in San Francisco. The Hoist in London. Le Keller in Paris. Quentin Crisp once said that gay men can be happy only when they realize there is no dark stranger waiting on a bar stool, waiting to love them, make them whole. But there are plenty of dark bars.

The men at the Böse Buben fix their faces in the same way men do in men's bars all over the world: mouths open and half-smiling but eyes stern and entrancingly unavailable. Some were too attentive, some wholly inattentive. The older men were small-eyed and clinging, the beautiful, shaved, and fit men were merciless, drinking beer from bottles with their elbows held high, their forearms like gauntlets. Those of us in the middle, men like me, looked about, back and forth across the bar, in and out of the groping rooms, all of us lonely or drunk or simply aware, aware of the wearing necessity of such places, such places and their rules. So be it. I fixed my face too.

There was Ben, a short man with enormous shoulders and powerful, muscular legs. He said he was an 'acktiv' (a top, in gay shorthand), but I had my doubts. His beard had been left to grow untrained, an afterthought, and his hair was curly, baby-fine. He was hardly gruff. He spoke like a junior-high music teacher. But what choice did he have? At fifty-six, he must become either a top, some bottom's 'onkel' (a daddy figure), or stay home at night for the rest of his life. Gay sex is like sports – you might make it to forty-five if you're lucky, then you have to become the coach or get out of the game. Ben did everything but wear a whistle around his neck.

And there was Manfred, who was so pale I couldn't judge his age. Sometimes he wore a black undershirt, and nothing else. Most of the time, he just wore nothing. He was tall and fit and boring. I thought he might be a mute, but he eventually whispered a few lies to me.

Walter had a beautiful backside, a rare and perfect pear still on the branch. The rest of him had gone to shit, dropped off the tree years ago, but no one misses whatever else Walter once offered, ever offered. He made a point of taking long, slow strides down the hall. The old bait-and-switch game.

I stood at the back of the club, always. Not quite the far back, the wall, but back enough, into the half-light, beside the idiotic candelabra, a wrought-iron boudoirism ornamented, of course, with chintz-red candles. I felt laughed at. Don't you need a bed to make a boudoir, I wondered. And a woman?

My face was fixed. It said: *I cannot be seduced, but I can be charmed.*

I met Alexandar at Blue Monday Pansexual Chillout Night at Quälgeist – basically, straight night. Boring straight-people night.

I was standing at the far wall of the playroom, behind the spiderweb rope net and a hanging leather body bag, the basic bondage jungle-gym set-up, and glaring at a limping middle-aged woman in a billowy black housedress and a leather dog collar as she wandered around the space methodically replacing the spent tea-light candles. Her black rubber slippers squeaked when she walked, *ee-aw, ee-aw, ee-aw*. I could have killed her.

But that was her job, tea light and (of course red) candle replacement. And snooping, hovering above the handful of couples who were bothering to have sex. Checking to see that nobody was being hurt – in an S&M club. I half expected her to come around with a tea trolley.

I felt about as sexy as a potted carnation.

And then there was Alexandar.

Alexandar was even more out of place than I was. He was wearing light blue dress trousers and a neatly pressed salmon-pink shirt. His brown hair was freshly cut (most of the men, even the balding ones, were marred by drooping, stringy pony-tails, never a good sign), his sideburns were razor-close to his cheeks, angled expertly downward, level with his earlobes, and he smelled of bergamot and cloves. His legs were thick with muscles, his thighs hard and high, like a cyclist's. His chest was wide and full, so was his belly. A cluster of curling hairs broke over the top button of his shirt. He kissed me without asking my name.

We went to the playroom and Alexandar sat me down on a low leather bench, placing first my left foot, then my right on the small pads attached to the wooden legs. I straddled the bench, my knees almost level with the main plank. I looked up at him, amused and curious. He stood closer, surveying me. Suddenly, he moved behind me and held my hands together in front of my chest. His grip was not so much powerful as it was concise. He gently pushed me down, laying my back lengthwise along the bench until my knees bent upward. The diaper position. I was prone, feet off the floor, legs unsteady, my fat back balancing on a narrow strip of leather and padding. I felt perfectly secure. I could fall only so far, after all.

Pinching my wrists together with one hand and holding them high above my head, Alexandar removed my jeans in four quick steps: belt undone, fly buttons popped, back belt loop grabbed, and seat yanked out from under me. I smiled, Alexandar smiled. Alexandar licked his index finger and forefinger and shoved both into my asshole. I tried to remember if he was wearing any rings, how long his nails were, but he was already inside, inside and making a V with his fingers, spreading my ass open.

Alexandar let go of my hands, and I placed both on my stomach. He shook his head. No, no. He took my right hand and plunked it roughly on top of my cock. 'Now,' he said, wiggling his buried fingers. 'Now.'

I pulled my cock up and down. I felt the hair on the back of his hand tickling my left thigh. I couldn't focus.

'Now,' he said again, his chin beside my ear. 'Now.'

I pulled my foreskin back tight, lifted my ass off the bench. Still, nothing.

Smiling, Alexandar swung his free hand over his head and landed it hard on the clenched lines of muscle between my upper legs and my ass cheeks. The sound of hand hitting rump was crisp and sharp, a sudden outburst of applause. The sting came a second later, and so did I.

Alexandar rubbed my belly and stood upright. He looked me up and down, his hand still inside my ass. He pulled out, wiped his fingers on my T-shirt, smirked at me, then fixed his shirt, tucking the shirttail in tight. He walked away.

I did not see Alexandar again for three weeks. I looked for him everywhere. Everywhere in Berlin a man who likes to put his fingers up another man goes for fun. Later, I would learn how much Alexandar disliked repetition, predictability, how he could never be the kind of man who enjoyed familiarity, a man who sought the comforts of a local watering hole, cultivated a set of usual haunts. At root (I do not say 'in his heart,' I will never speak of hearts, I do not believe in the heart), Alexandar did not have any essential human needs. Not even the basics: comfort, conviviality, affection. I wondered at times if he ever ate. I never saw him eat. I never saw him scratch himself, never heard his stomach rumble. His skin never broke out with pimples or stray hairs. He was never sweaty or musky. Alexandar was not a man, he was the presence of a man. Only that. And that was all I wanted. Until I wanted more.

In Berlin I lived a life completely free of routine, schedules, or appointments, the opposite of my life in Toronto. In Berlin, no two days were the same. Except for the screaming boy.

A young family with three children, Goran and Jessica and kids one, two, and three, lived two floors above me. All the children were boys. The oldest was perhaps seven, the youngest about three. I met them only once, but I heard them, heard him, the howler, every day, every late afternoon between six and six thirty.

Jessica or Goran arrived home from work, all three boys in tow. The older boys would run up the stairs. Jessica or Goran checked the mailbox, fumbled for keys, tried to get the boys to haul bags up the stairs, all the while leaving the baby sitting in his stroller. From the moment the baby was left on his own, only a few feet away from his family, he began to scream. Really scream. Not a begging half cry, the kind babies learn to perform, the kind with no tears, but a guttural, wretched, tortured scream. The courtyard and the lobby echoed with his rage.

Jessica or Goran maybe thought they were teaching their baby about independence, not realizing that suddenly, in his baby mind, the boy was abandoned. He could not see his parent, his magic flying brothers. The lobby was cold and dark. The sunny courtyard behind the lobby – full of flowers and cats, later fresh snow and icicles and cats – shone in front of him, just beyond a pair of tall, windowed doors, full of wonders. Too far away, everything was too far away.

Forty-five seconds. Forty-five seconds from clumsy, bustling, everyday family noises, from boyish chitters and chirps and low, shushing maternal sounds, from nothing to notice, nothing but just children growing up, children racing up stairs, children jostling and burping and slamming doors … to the purest, hardest, most succinct expression of hate, true hate, that I ever heard or want to hear again. That's all it took. Forty-five seconds. But it lasted long after. Once for an hour, all throughout the building, rounds and rounds of wailing.

Can you blame me for casting a spell, a mild curse? Every damned day. The child was not human, it could not be. A human child would grow hoarse, tired, cry itself sick.

I began to watch for the little family, hide behind my front window, blink out of the peephole in my front door. I wanted to see the baby's face, see his horns.

Once, I did. Well, not horns. I caught his gaze.

He was standing upright in the stroller, his hands clutching the back of the seat, his mouth wide open. Somehow, he was inhaling and hollering at the same time. His face was hot red from the forehead up, his fat cheeks were blue and purple, his mouth a cold white, lips two wriggling maggots. Yes, I hated him that much.

We looked at each other, him with both eyes, me with one eye, my glasses off, one weak eye straining through the peephole. The soles of my feet began to itch, then tingle, then burn. The tiles under my feet changed colour, from a harmless beige to a watery, marbled black. I jumped back, terrified and certain. Not human. I double-locked my door, and did so every day after.

The next morning, when I was sure that all the working tenants were out of the building, I took a box of salt and poured a little pile into each corner of the lobby. I made a trap. Four tiny white pyramids. Since the lobby was never cleaned, I knew they would hold. Hold him at bay.

Let him call up Hell itself, I thought, I'm protected. Let him unleash great snakes, the twenty thousand whores of Babylon, lions with nine heads and rams with diamonds for eyes. Let him turn day to night; I've created a perimeter, a safe quadrant, a spell of enclosure.

When the little family came home that night, I heard the usual parade of shuffling and whining, then the jingle of keys and the brisk clapping of small feet against worn wooden steps, then the mumbled parental cautions, then the first, searching cry, followed by the irritated snarl, the warm-up before the five-alarm assault.

He did his best, the little shit. The inhuman little shit. He made a choir of his voice, brought in new notes, new voices, baritones and tenors and a smoky speak-sing croak. He added instruments (a whistle, a trio of tuning forks, a rattlesnake's rattle) and effects (the sound of a chair leg breaking, the scrape of a straight razor on the back of a neck, a caw), played noise against note, song against chaos. I was not moved. I did not go to my door. I did not run the kitchen tap to block out his incantations. I did not cover my head with pillows. I did not sigh, stomp about, or turn up the radio. I listened and laughed.

I could never kill a child, I told myself. But that is not a child. *And all I am doing is letting his fingers come close to the fire.*

The morning after I met Alexandar, I sat on the floor of my living room and read Tarot cards, spread after spread of messages and signs. Because I did not believe in love.

In every reveal, a nine-card spread or a fourteen-card spread or a two-card flash cast, one or two or all three of three particular cards returned. Finally, I removed them from the deck and shuffled them independently, to determine their hierarchy, their floating message. They arrived in this order:

Knight of Pentacles. Five of Swords. King of Swords.

The five swords are arranged in a pentacle. Thus, two pentacles: the Five in the Five of Swords and the pentacle held aloft by the Knight of Pentacles. Read duality, connection. And two brandishings of swords: in the Five of Swords, in a star shape, like a shield, and in the King of Swords, a seated monarch who shows the flat of the blade, because power lies in not having to mention the cutting edge, the stabbing tip. Read, a rage for dominance. Between two men. Which was which?

The pentacle is a five-pointed star made with one continuous line that turns in five directions. Beginning and end and beginning again, the outside reiterates the inside but the inside remakes the whole. The pentacle is an uneven bargain, a deal struck with a cheat.

The King of Swords holds his broadsword in his right hand and a holy book in his left hand. Left, the hand demonic. The Knight of Pentacles is a small man riding an enormous horse. His helmet is winged, his boots are spurred and shaped like curved sickles, talons. He holds a disc bearing a pentacle above his head, again in the left hand, the hand demonic.

The Knight of Pentacles is covered head to foot in crisp armour, the King of Swords is draped in two long cloaks. The Knight of Pentacles could be a boy. His face is dimpled, his nose elfin. The King of Swords is a man. His face shows the start of jowls, a downward pull.

Two men of affiliated but different rank. Two men carrying totems, holy or forbidden or both, in their left hands. Two men united by a star, a star drawn with an unbroken line, a star made out of swords.

The Five of Swords is both a promise and a warning. The promise: easy, perhaps eternal, connection. The unbroken line. The warning: five upon five upon five blades, double-sided. No end of tears. A death by cuts.

Never again would any of these three cards appear to me, never individually and certainly never together. It was as if the cards, exasperated with me, were crying out, *What more do you want? If you're going to be an idiot, after all, leave us! Go stare at wet tea leaves, spin red wine around a black plate, cast bones and sticks on the floor, look under the bottoms of rocks! Read your own spit! Catch a dove, cut out its liver, translate the bruises. Leave us.*

How obvious it all is now. An abundance of metals. Invasion, assault. Transmutation through force, force and fire, hammers and heat. But gold equals purity, things irreducible. Silver is sister to gold. The sun and the moon. Everything is changeable, or everything is set, predetermined.

I laughed and cut the deck into three unequal piles. I placed the King on top of one pile, the Five on the second, and the Prince on the third. I gathered the cards together in counter-order, pile number two on top of pile number one, then the bottom of pile number three on top of pile number two. I shuffled and reshuffled, then rolled a creased blue paper bag, a leftover from a pricey Bergmanstrasse gift shop, around the deck twice. I bound the bundle with a thick green rubber band.

I sat on the floor, stared at the ceiling, and absently snapped the rubber band while, above my head, someone filled a sink or flushed a toilet or got a glass of water. The pipes did their clumsy dance. A hunk of plaster, the size and weight of a half-euro coin, popped off the ceiling and landed at my feet, like a present. *Someday*, I thought, *this whole building will turn itself inside out.* I needed some air, new faces, a bottle of cheap liqueur.

The cards sat untouched for weeks after, sulking underneath a mystery novel and a German-English dictionary. I had so many other things to do.

I have had sex in many strange places. A Montreal dockyard warehouse storing thousands of bags of dog kibble and squeaking rats. An antique dealer's coach house in east Toronto that was so packed with cherry-coloured glass globe oil lamps that we had to tiptoe on paths marked with electrical tape to get to the bedroom. A lean-to in a forest outside Fredericton. A bathhouse decorated in pink and banana-yellow floral wallpaper, run by two Portuguese guys who refused to turn down the shrieking Brazilian soap opera playing on a massive television located inches away from my cabin. A bathhouse under a bridge in London with wet, black-green mould growing on the stone walls. No end of cars, vans, trucks, and the backs of trucks, in front seats and back seats, in opened hatchbacks, in locked taxis. Parks, parkettes, patches of brush, along riverbanks and at the bottoms of gravel pits. In tiny rented rooms, and, of course, in hotels. While families ate dinner a floor above me, oblivious, while senile mothers watched *Jeopardy!* in the basement below, calling out answers. In porn theatre cabins in Paris, in front of straight porn in a bungalow in Whitby. Over the phone.

I am not bragging. Most of these situations became exciting or ironically glamorous only after the fact. Often, at the time, I just felt stupid and detached. But not always. A thrill's a thrill.

From the moment I entered Harald and Max's house, I knew I would have to rearrange my Top Ten list. Harald and Max lived in a madhouse. A madhouse of their own design.

I met Harald and Max online (I want to write 'Harald & Max,' because it was how they always spoke of themselves, in a clipped manner that revealed decades of living together, in a way that made you visualize the ampersand forever between them). It took three sets of negotiations to set up a meeting – fairly fast for online dating. Harald and Max were not about to waste time, and when I got to their home I understood why – they had decorating to do. Decorating on top of decorating.

Harald and Max lived in Bernau, an hour's S-Bahn ride north of central Berlin. Bernau was a tiny enclave of Old Germany, a farm town complete with two wood-panelled beer halls, three smoky asparagus-and-sausage restaurants, a bowling alley (*Germans bowl?* I thought), plenty of suspicious old people, people trained to watch, always watch, rows of timber-and-tile gable-front houses, and a sweetly scented, humming swamp, likely full of bones.

Harald met me at the S station. He was very tall, over six feet five, and well over his stated age of fifty-three. His eyebrows were as thick as mitten thumbs and grew in all directions. He had a lovely smile, a laughing smile. He spoke almost no English. We walked in silence to his house, down a quiet road lined with early-twentieth-century farmhouses, low-to-the-ground, stucco-slathered buildings with high-pointed witch-hat roofs.

We turned down a weed-strewn alley and there was Max, little Max. Five feet three inches tall, bulky and cherub-faced, with bright grey hair. Max was the baby of this little family, the baby with silver hair.

Max led us to their front gate, a handmade, tilting structure made of old, dry linden branches, a few squares of chicken wire, old dry rope and new, still-springy rope, and cascading vines, grape vines and clematis vines and speckled ivy. The gate was locked with a combination lock that had never been dialled, been left to rust open. Along the top of the gate, I saw the first signs of Harald and Max's distinctive decorating style: a series of black heads rested on sticks. Sculpted from papier mâché and slathered in tar, the guardians included an owl, a gargoyle, a lion, a howling gargoyle, in the style of Munch's *The Scream*, and a curly haired cupid with a necklace of bent arrows.

And that was nothing. Harald and Max loved papier mâché. Every inch of their massive farmhouse, an open barn of a building with a ceiling two storeys above the main floor, was transformed by paper and paste. To pull open a cabinet or pass through a door, you had to grasp a tab or a doorknob that had been turned into an open-mouthed Pan or a leafy Green Man. Sit on a chair, and the arms, back, and legs encircled you in tentacles, or horns, or outcroppings of nettle leaves. Lampshades and sconces and pendant light fixtures were remade into spiky crowns, complete with embedded plastic jewels, upside-down trees with roots spreading across the ceiling, and flaming torches (in bright orange tissue paper). Light switches were, of course, erect penises. Such fun! The backboard of their bed was four times its original size, an attempt to replicate Picasso's *Guernica* in alternating shades of brown parcel paper, brick-red butcher paper, and washed-out newsprint. The entrance to the sex room was a two-panel door, opening outward. A massive hell mouth was plastered over the panels, done in beige paper. To suggest skin, I figured.

The sex room itself was a total disappointment. A narrow bed, unadorned. A school desk, for teacher-student games, also unadorned, and a pillory, a plain, unvarnished wood pillory, made from common two-by-fours and iron bolts. The floor was newly covered in sparkling, forest-green tile. The room smelled of lemon cleanser. Some dungeon, I thought. Some hell.

The actual sex hardly lived up to the decor. It was as dull as the room promised. First, Harald played the school headmaster. I was bent over the desk. He fingered me for a few moments while Max watched from the other side of the room. Max, Harald told me, had a bit of a cold that day. Max eventually roused himself and gestured for me to lean against the pillory, face out. He sucked me vigorously for ten or fifteen minutes, snuffling and coughing the whole time, then gave up. Harald finished me off back at the school desk. At least he was tall enough to pull off the headmaster routine. I kept waiting for one or both of them to slide on papier-mâché Devil masks, or, better yet, violate me with a papier-mâché phallus, a monster phallus, with horns and spikes. No such luck.

Afterwards, we sat in their untended garden and Harald made polite but necessarily fragmented conversation. Max said nothing. Was he upset or was his mind just elsewhere? I noticed Max kept looking at his rangy, never-pruned apple tree. Perhaps he was thinking of Adam and Eve under the Tree of Knowledge, and how much paper and glue he would need to create statues of them. Where to place the Snake?

Harald said, 'Canada is a very liberal country.'

'Not lately,' I replied.

Max stared at the apple tree.

'No, this is because why no?' Harald asked.

I shrugged. *Bad times*, my face said. Harald nodded.

Suddenly, Max stood up and motioned for me to follow him across the garden to a massive mound of dirt. At the foot of the mound, buckets filled with gravel and mud waited. Max picked up a bucket, motioned for me to do the same. We stumbled up to the top of the mound and dumped out our buckets. Then Max bumbled back down. I followed, completely confused.

Harald said, 'This is Max game. Every boy who comes to garden must make the mountain one bucket tall more.' He laughed.

I looked again at the mound. It was at least a dozen feet tall. One fuck bucket at a time.

Harald and Max told me to come back any time I wanted. Well, Harald did. Come for dinner, come for a bike ride to the river, come for Oktoberfest, come for skiing, sleep in the guest-room (done up as a magic forest, with giant toadstools for end tables and a bed recast as a lilypad), know us – we are your new friends in Germany.

I never saw them again.

I'm compiling a record of the men I have had sex with in Berlin, counting from day one. I'm perverse in the true sense – I want to remember as perfectly as possible things it would probably be better to forget, things I can never feel or do again, because it gives me pleasure to have unnecessary knowledge to hand. A pervert knows too much.

Böse Buben (bad baby, I think, or bad boys – more kinder culture!): Very cheap beer, nobody under thirty-five as far as I could tell. White candles everywhere. Sex in Berlin is never very far in feel from a fussy dinner party.

Quälgeist 'SklavenNacht' (Slave Night): Men self-segregated at the door as either 'masters' or 'slaves.' Masters went to the bar, slaves were forced to strip naked and wait in a cold anteroom. Slaves were given a number and a form to fill out, the form detailing what they would do or not do with the masters (piss, fisting, etc.), and then the form was tied around their necks. Eventually all the slaves were paraded in front of the masters, and the masters took their pick. I opted for 'Sklave,' thought I could try 'Meister' next time. I was picked second-last, just before a grizzled senior in his seventies. My 'Meister': five feet, eleven inches, forty-five or so. Massive muscle man gone to chubby seed; thin beard and tell-tale 'AIDS face' dimples on his cheeks. Angry top. Took two 'slaves' at once. Greedy and in a hurry. Left immediately after.

Böse Buben Lederhosen Nacht (leather shorts 'Bavarian' night): Leather shorts are for schoolboys, all schoolboys need caning. Apparently a Bavarian fetish. No Name 2: six feet tall, forty-three. Unreconstructed 1970s moustache leatherman: chaps, biker chain, Muir cap. Beautiful sinewy legs and a slow smile. Slight build but strong as two oxen. Lifted me off the ground several times, pushed my face into his crotch until my nose bent. Marius: six feet, three inches, forty. Enormous man, Norwegian high school principal. Bull-chested, beer-bellied. Threw me over a pommel horse (Böse Buben has a collection of vintage gymnastic equipment, for no evident decorative reason) and fingered me until I was open, then took off his belt and inserted the round buckle. I bought him a beer. At midnight, plates of oversized pretzels and 'white sausage' were passed around. Marius ate five. Five plates.

Quälgeist: Boss (self-nicknamed): five feet, five inches, over sixty. Napoleon complex. Weird, Ming the Merciless eyebrows. Idiot. Boss, working the coat check, tells me after that he's seen my picture on GayRomeo.com and that I am now 'at least forty kilos fatter' (half true). Fucking cunt.

Böse Buben Christmas Party: Awful. Totally off my game. Brief topping by Idiot 1: five feet, eleven inches, forty-seven. Forget-table features. And Idiot 2: five feet, seven inches, about thirty-five. Human blank page. Gave up after I saw one guy I thought was cute – glasses, five feet, nine inches, about forty, cop moustache, stocky build – so said hello to him and he ran away. Literally ran. Merry Christmas.

Scheune: New Year atmosphere. Storm clouds of frantic, pre-quitting-in-the-new-year cigarette smoke. Muscle Papa: five feet, seven inches, fifty-five. Bearded, built like a bull. Rubber Nutter: five feet, eleven inches, thirty-three or younger. Head-to-toe rubber gear that smelled like cooking oil. Ulli: five feet, eleven inches, just under forty. Met first on GayRomeo.com. Pug-faced rough gear freak. Deep, dirty fucking.

Quälgeist employs Berlin's cuntiest bartender. A lizard in track pants. Oily tan flamer, but without the charm. My friend J kept calling him 'Darling' until he screamed 'Mein nommen ist Wolf-gang!!' Wolfgang Darling has a voice like a flayed ferret.

My apartment: Dom_Tom. GayRomeo.com find. Five feet, nine inches, or a little taller. Showed up in a crisp, tight-fitting suit. Fifty-five years old, built like a thirty-five-year-old athlete. Gorgeous, well-groomed businessman. And nasty. Bruising nasty. Breath control/choking nasty. I could not stop feeling his biceps and full chest. A bulldog of a man. Best two hours in Berlin. And then he got weird, sulky and needy. I had to prepare a meal for him, and then coffee, and then dessert. And he wanted to stay overnight and made a big production of having to leave. The coldest, hardest men always display the most childlike needs. Crestfallen again, scuffed knees again, ready for more.

Quälgeist: The Most Beautiful Young Man in the World. Five feet, eleven inches, thirty. Blond and perfect beach-bunny guy. Skin smooth as tulip petals. An angel. High as a tower. Wanted me to chase him, literally, all around the club, up the stairs and into the dark corners. So I did. Finally caught him and finger-fucked him. A quart of cum was my reward.

Robert the Dutch Muscle Daddy (repeat): Six feet, five inches, over sixty. Muscles on top of muscles, short grey hair, full lips, the proverbial leather harness. Great kisser and abrasive bondage top. Tied me to a post and had his way. Sweet man.

Quälgeist: Worst misuse of fifteen euros. Just under twenty guys in the whole club, and all of them apparently went to high school together. Wolfgang Darling attending bar and spitting into the drinks. Nothing is as abject as a bar full of 'regulars.' Wolfgang Darling barked at me twice for not speaking German. And then two very pretty Scottish boys entered, and he was suddenly as fluent in the Queen's English as Stephen Fry. *Free schnapps for the Scots!* How I hate that cunt. Finally, scored Banker Dad: just under six feet tall, just under fifty. Athletic type, gone to seed but still energetic. Dressed in business casual, he was wonderfully out of place. He carried a wooden spoon in his briefcase and spanked me with it, which I found hilarious. A true freak. Wolfgang Darling watched us, his lips curling like a frightened eel in a shallow pond. How easy it would be to wait in the dark courtyard beside the club until Wolfgang Darling toddled off for home. How quickly I could cut his scrawny throat. His blood would taste like bitters, piss, and rancid olives.

Whatever I may now think or write or remember about Alexandar, bad and good, remember now, from my quiet, bleached, and insulated little ledge, this safety that is for my own good, Alexandar can be blamed for only so much. He untied every knot inside me, but the rope was snarled long before I met him. It's coiling again.

Loneliness is the easiest emotion to bear. Loneliness hides, sleeps, tucks itself between the vital organs. Alchemists believed loneliness resided in the liver. Loneliness is the opposite of rage – it demands no action, no vent. Loneliness can live inside you for decades, like an accidentally swallowed pebble of glass or a piece of razor that the skin has grown over and dulled, let sink into the underside of a muscle. Loneliness has no wants. And then it does. And then you are sick with it, falling-to-the-floor sick, aching and retching. You will do anything to be rid of the sudden invasion, the invasion you could have heard coming if only you'd put your ear to the rail, like a common idiot, could have seen it assembling its troops if only you'd taken a hilltop now and then, just been brave and reckless, less clever.

No, that is not accurate. Loneliness is not exclusively a coward's disease, or only a bookish dilemma. It strikes mountaineers and moles alike. It's convenient for me to think of myself as being prone to loneliness, as having an innate, unavoidable tendency to be lonely, a genetic flaw, a character impairment. But the truth is simpler: I was lazy, things came to me easily, and I thought love was for people who couldn't entertain themselves. I was proud of being alone in the world. Cocky and sneering. I was one of those people who, if asked, *Do you want to die alone?*, always answered, *Yes, Yes I do. Yes I do, and wide awake.*

Alexandar did not come to me easily, and that was most of his charm. He once asked me why I had been alone all my adult life, and when I replied with some bit of flippancy, something clever and thin, he cried. Men who are quick-witted, he said, reminded him of his father, who was sharp and fast with a joke and cruel as a razor.

The second time I saw Alexandar was at Franken, the oldest, dirtiest punk bar in East Berlin. Franken smelled like the bottom of a burned ashtray and look like an abandoned home that had been taken over by angry squatters, squatters packing black felt markers and carving knives. Even the urinals were covered in tags, beyond bleach. Once every other month, the bar shut down for a day while the staff, armed with power sprayers, slathered the piss stalls with white paint. If you bored a hole into the layers, you'd find bits of stickers and pen scratches dating from the first wave of punk in the 1970s, on to the robotic new-wave era, then to the ska craze, to death-metal triumphalism, to rap-rock, and then back again, to the retro-punk of the end of the century. Franken was about as gay-friendly as a prison riot.

But there was Alexandar. I was following a gang of straight painter guys around town, hiding behind one of the larger ones every time a fight broke out or the cops burst in to haul out a petty thief or dealer. I felt perfectly safe. But there was Alexandar, belly to the bar, calm as an armed guard. He was wearing thin dark-blue wool pants, perfectly pressed, and a navy blue shirt, flatter and smoother than a shield. I wondered if he had an ascot in his pocket.

'Is this your, um, local?' I asked.

'I'm comfortable everywhere.'

'You look comfortable.'

'Try me.'

Four minutes later, we were in the alley behind the bar. Alexandar lifted the front of my baggy T-shirt over my head and pulled the bunched fabric down my back, binding my arms to my shoulders. He bit my right nipple and twisted my left between his thumb and forefinger. When I began to unbutton my jeans, he slapped my hand away and pressed his elbow against my crotch, lightly at first and then with more force. I began to double over, but he leaned into me, holding me upright.

A swarm of drunk American college kids wandered past us, arguing the merits of Henry James vs. Poe. First-year excitements. They watched us for a moment, their pretty heads tilted toward the end of the alley, watched us with the same half attention you would give ducks floating on a river, or flies chasing each other, or one dog stupidly humping another. One kid started to laugh, but the boys shushed her and they moved on, back to Poe and then probably Plath and then maybe the state of the EU, and should their parents buy property in Spain.

My glasses fell off my face and landed between an empty pocket-sized bottle of schnapps and an abandoned paper plate smothered in fries and ketchup. Alexandar pulled on my nipples, pulled them straight out, a warning to stay still, then bent down and picked up my glasses. The rims were clotted with ketchup. He put them back on my face and smiled.

'You look like a little retarded boy,' he said.

That's not funny, I thought, as he undid the front of my pants. *That's not funny that's shitty that's creepy that's not how I like to be talked to that's not sexy.* My cock was in his hand. *I'm going to stop now he's a psycho I'm getting out of here there's rough and then there's too rough.* He pumped my cock, made a fist around it. Three short tugs, then one long pull. Three short, one long. Three short, one long. *I'm done with this*, I thought, and stayed perfectly still.

'You're charming,' he said, 'and so clever.'

One long pull, and I came all over his hands. He licked his thumb, then kissed both of my nipples, wetting them with his tongue and giving each one a little play bite.

'And which side are you on?' he asked, stepping back.

I struggled to get my T-shirt back over my chest. I couldn't find the hole for my head. My pants were undone, my face was sugared with ketchup, more people were rolling past the alley, and I was tangled in my own clothes. Alexandar watched. I got the T-shirt over my head and he pulled me close to him, shielding me as the drunks stumbled past. I did up my pants. Alexandar turned back to the bar, fishing in his pocket for money.

'Well, which side? What is it, Martin: James or Poe?'

'Hawthorne.'

'You're so clever, ketchup face.'

An hour later, Alexandar was so drunk he couldn't stand, he could only lean into things. I was too drunk to leave my seat. I wanted to eat, and then vomit, and then eat again, but I'd have to get up from my chair to do any of that. So there we stayed until the sun closed the bar. I don't remember how I got back to my apartment. I don't remember which direction Alexandar took when he walked away. I don't remember if we said goodbye or kissed goodbye or even if we left together. All I was good for over the next twenty-four hours was a long bath and watching, for the third time, *Ball of Fire*, starring Barbara Stanwyck and Gary Cooper. It's a comedy about a chorus girl who falls in love with a professor of grammar. Which side was I on?

In the tub, I rubbed astringent soap on my nipples. The left was bruised, the right beginning to cover in a hard layer of skin, like a heel. The hot water streamed out of the faucet slowly, reluctantly, in bubbles and drips, accompanied by a deep, subterranean barking sound. I watched the mirror over the sink cloud up, the waves of steam form shapes on the glass. A half face, a leg, the roots of a tree, a near-complete triangle, a zigzag line, like children make to draw waves under pirate ships, a peach-cleft backside, fern leaves.

I let my face sink under the soapy, stinging water. I turned my head to the left and went down. Water filled my ear canal, made a gentle pop inside my skull. I came up for air and did the same on the right side. Now I was deaf. *Let every piece of metal in the house sing,* I thought. *I can't hear them anymore.*

'Oh, Canada,' Germans always say, 'it is my dream to go to Canada.' Or, 'I have been in Canada. I have been in Toronto. Toronto is a good place to live, yes?' They don't know shit. Their Canada is a fantasy, a woodland haven, Snow White's forest. I would like to live there myself. And their Toronto is clean and bright and free of old ideas. I tried to live there and failed.

I left Toronto for so many reasons and one very simple one: I could no longer stand myself. How I got to this point of self-loathing was far from simple, however, as are most things in Toronto. The city eats at you, kicks you in your sleep, drips cold water on your feet. You don't notice it at first, the pestering. You think it's just urban life, the trade-off for living large. But eventually reality dawns on you – the particular reality of living in the largest city of a leftover colony – that you will never be good enough. The centre is always elsewhere. You are second-rate in the First World. No amount of effort or imagination can cure this realization. The thin, pleading boosterism fostered by the local media, the endless series of 'city-building' panel discussions, idiotic sports pride: none of it ever silences the low, exhausted sigh of defeat that exhales from every tired face, new building, or bestseller. You can't sing away a fog, pat a back with no bones.

I wrote a weekly column for a large newspaper, after years of working sporadically and in poverty for very small newspapers. I was forty-seven years old and at my peak. Seven hundred and fifty dollars a week, but only if I managed to grind out a column. No vacation, no vacation pay, no prescription, glasses, or dental benefits. No union protection, no security, no pension. Twenty-five years into a profession, and I was less valuable to my employers than the women who vacuumed the office every night. And I was considered one of the lucky ones, a writer who had written his way to the top. At forty-seven, to be so underwhelmed …

Worse yet, I often thought of myself as a person who had done well in life, as someone who had earned a standing in my community. I believed the Toronto lie. To be nothing is one thing, to be nothing and deluded another. I faced two choices: continue on and wake up at fifty-five or sixty and realize that second-best only ever degrades to third- or fourth-best, and then to entirely absent, or continue on until the newspaper realized I could be replaced by anybody half my age at one-third my pay, and then be left adrift, adrift to watch all the people who paid me so much attention drop me for the new boy.

Why not, I asked myself, why not just leave? Run away to someplace where nobody knows you and drink and fuck yourself to death? To fail in a city where you don't know the rules of success, don't even understand the native language, would be so much easier than collapsing in a city with borrowed ideas of success, where failure is judged more harshly because the very idea of accomplishment is itself second-hand.

And writing for newspapers makes you morbid. Or, to be fair, morbid people find a neat outlet in newspapers. Journalism is reactive, not creative. A journalist is always apart, in the crowd but never in the crush, neither in danger nor dangerous. A journalist is either born half-dead inside or very quickly learns to live with only half his internal organs. A journalist in not a vital person, in body or pursuits. I often spent whole days in bed, thinking up opening lines for my column. In another era, I'd have been a monk charged with illuminating one book of the Bible – and that would be it, my life's work. I would have had no name.

I looked for Alexandar everywhere. Everywhere I thought he should be: in any venue, ridiculous to menacing, where a man in Berlin would meet other ridiculous and dangerous men, or just the lonely.

I looked for Alexandar in the places I assumed he frequented, the sex bars that tried so hard, too hard, to create a kind of toughness, an intentionally limited idea of maleness, all saddle leather and beer bottles, wood panelling and concrete floors, black on grey on black.

I looked for Alexandar in bars and clubs where I would see the same men over and over, and I had been in Berlin for only a month. I thought that meant I was on the right path, that I was among the veterans, already deeply connected to the casual sex scene, an insider. But I would never be an insider. There is no such thing.

I looked for Alexandar behind doors only an idiot would not be embarrassed to pass through, and Alexandar was hardly an idiot. That much I knew already. But a romantic mission is nothing if not humiliating. I knew I was on the wrong track, in all the wrong places, and I carried on, going back for seconds and thirds. I know now that what I was trying to do was find another Alexandar, convince myself there was nothing special about him, that Alexandars were mine for the picking at any boots-and-underwear party, spanking-and-dildo night, sadomasochism (with free buffet) genderqueer-and-trans salon. This city, I told myself, is full of men worth falling over. This city, I told myself, will open up at my feet and I will be in love ten times, a dozen times, one hundred times. This city will be the happy death of me, Alexandar be damned.

Whatever you dream, you make real. The Devil is a better listener than God.

Throughout the fall, and twice in December – two days before Christmas and a week after Christmas – letters arrived from Russia. I got as many as four in one week, sometimes three at once, sometimes only one letter in a tiny, business-card-sized envelope. I knew they were from Russia by the stamps. The letters were addressed to a name written in Cyrillic, with only my apartment and street number written in clumsy, block-capital German. None of the letters contained a return address, but the handwriting was obviously the same, from the hand of a very nervous person. Or a person writing in their sleep. The pen moved across the rough envelope paper with impatience, leaving smears of ink between the spindly, thread-thin, but never touching, never flowing together bits of alphabet.

At first, the lost letters charmed me. Surely, someone would come for his or her mail eventually. Meanwhile, I had a cute mystery on my hands. But by the time the letters took up more desk space than my laptop and I'd run out of bundling elastic bands, I decided they were detestable, sad, perhaps the works of a psychotic, a stalker. I wanted rid of them but couldn't just throw them away. *What*, I thought, *what if someone was desperately trying to reach me and an inconsiderate person tossed all the messages away? I would be furious.*

I asked around the building. It was as if the previous tenant had never existed. My fellow tenants with children, the bulk of them, were always too distracted, too busy chasing one whinging brat after the next, to even look at the letters. The grumpy, unreconstructed Marxist hippies across the hall, a couple in their late fifties who insisted on leaving their foul-smelling sandals on a rack outside their front door – the Ponytail Twins, I called them – opened their door cautiously, then saw the bundle of mail in my hand and recoiled. He shouldered me away with his tall, lumpy body, blocking the door frame and forcing me backward, off their cheery straw Willkommen mat. *No*, he said, *no, not us. Not for us. We don't want them.*

I looked up the German word for 'moved away' – weggehen – and marked each envelope, over thirty by then, in big black letters. I stuffed the lot in the nearest mailbox. Every single one of them came back, followed by new letters. Once, I caught the Deutsche Post man cramming more of the miserable packets into my mailbox and I told him I was not that person, that whoever this Russian was, they were no longer living here. He shrugged his huge shoulders, stared at me for many more seconds than I was comfortable with, and then put two more envelopes into my box.

Curiosity got the better of me only once. I opened one letter. I told myself that I wanted to save the beautiful, oversized stamps: three rectangles decorated with images of Russian birds. The borders of the stamps glinted with bright, copper-coloured metallic paper. I told myself I would cut the stamps off the envelope and never read the letter inside. I told myself one opened letter in a mountain of letters was no great sin. I told myself that there was no such thing as bad luck.

The envelope contained one piece of paper, covered with text and diagrams on both sides, and, in the creases where the paper had been folded and refolded, a soft, talc-like turquoise powder that smelled of cloves. The powder instantly stuck to the tips of my fingers and would not brush off. Maybe it was poison? I rushed to the sink and washed my hands in scalding water.

I put two shoes on my desk and gently unfolded the letter again with the tip of a pencil. I weighted the bottom of the page with one shoe, then the top with another. I had no idea if I was looking at the first or second half of the letter, or if it mattered, if the letter contained any logic of its own, any start or finish. Even if I could not read Russian, I knew insanity when I saw it.

The handwriting was steady, aggressive. The ink was common, ballpoint black. Individual letters within words never touched, and the spaces between the words were exactly the same from word to word, sentence to sentence. It was as if the writer had used a ruler to keep the lines and the information on the lines in a precise, predetermined order. Some sentences were repeated, with the same exaction, but backwards. I counted eleven such reversals. Fragments of text ran up and down the margins, enclosed in blocks of identical, beautifully drawn eight-point stars.

Despite the evident meticulousness, the letter appeared to have been written in a hurry. The reversed sentences broke through the page, creating tufts, wave crests, of white paper. The ink had not had time to dry before the writer carried on to the next phrase, often the next letter, leaving smear marks where a palm had brushed against wet ink, where a thumb nudged too close to a wet L or E. I guessed that the writer was right-handed but had used his (I also guessed the writer was male) left hand to craft the letter – the better to fool the reader. Or protect himself.

Taking up the pencil and the shoes, I flipped the page over. The same person could not have crafted the two sides. The hand that covered the paper before me was shaky, panicked, and utterly mad, incapable of making straight lines. The paper was not covered, it was carved. Carved with symbols, single words written back to front, then front to back, accidental, watery fingerprints, marks from moments when the writer had intentionally smeared the paper with his nails, drops of red wax, and clumsy mustard stains. The paper smelled of pork fat and wet tobacco, of stale tea.

I counted 117 symbols, some as small as the head of a finishing nail, half a dozen as big as two-euro coins. Stars, four-point and nine-point and ten-point, but never a five-pointed star, splotchy asterisks, flower shapes, arabesques, animals (a lion, a dog, a rat, a worm or headless snake), circles encircling eyes, the letter X surrounded by grinning skulls, thirty-three faces, no two alike in features or expression, an axe with a clean blade, an axe dripping blood, an ear so carefully drawn I thought at first the drawing had been cut out of an anatomy textbook and pasted onto the page, and, largest of all, a triangle with a long, curling, and hairy tail.

When I was in university, I had a roommate, G, who suffered from *horror vacui*, a fear of empty or unmarked spaces and surfaces. He simply could not leave a blank piece of paper alone. The other students made G the subject of a cruel pub game. As did I. Once everyone was on their way to being roaring drunk, someone would pull a fresh piece of white paper out of their knapsack, or, in a pinch, turn a cardboard coaster over, blank face up, and casually leave the bait in front of G.

Whoever was closest to G would ask to borrow a pen. G always had a pen on him. Then, we waited as G grew increasingly anxious. He could not take his eyes off the clean paper. From this point, the game was simple: whoever kept from sipping until G finally snapped and hollered for his pen back was off the hook for rounds for the rest of the night. On nights when everyone was flush with their monthly student allowance cheques, the game took a more cutthroat turn: the drinker with a glass to their lips or their drink in their hands when G flipped out had to pay the tab at the end of the night.

We played this game for an entire term, until one night G started to cry. I had his pen. I was laughing at some joke. G turned to me, tears bubbling down his cheeks, and whispered, *Please. Please.* He was shaking with rage – not at me, but at himself, at his weakness, at being cursed with a pointless compulsion, a drive that he could neither harness nor gain from.

After that, we always made sure there was plenty of fresh paper and a pen for G, at the cafeteria, at the pub, in the coffee shop, even at the movies, in case the film snapped and the screen went blank. A girl in the history department gave him a set of coloured pencils for Christmas. I bet he loves her to this day, in his helpless fashion. G is a recluse now. Just like me, except his seclusion is voluntary. G gets the last laugh.

The crazed letter from Russia, naturally, reminded me of G, and I dreamed of him that night.

He was drawing an enormous picture of a cable bridge on a sparkling white wall. The Golden Gate Bridge, or a good facsimile. His shoulders were hunched around his neck, as if he was being blasted from behind by a cold wind. He never faced me. His hands were ridiculously large, the size of turkey platters. His nails were filthy, clotted with hair and mud and something soft and spongy, like antler felt. He used a smooth grey rock, a beach stone, for a pencil.

It appears that I can live on memories. I suppose I must.

My room, my cell, is a projector's booth and the blank walls are screens. I fill them day and night with detailed visions, beautifully art-directed reconstructions. It is easy work.

My mind refuses to be occupied with the official distractions I'm offered: the four meals a day, the half-hour solitary walk inside the fading, bone-dry walled garden (how much less gloomy it would be if it were left to return to mud, without the idiotic, done-on-the-cheap landscaping, the common gorse and bent, failing linden tree), the glint of sunlight on razor wire that is brighter than any flower, and, of course, the mandatory monthly 'chats' with psychiatrists, little farces of conviviality wherein it is determined not how sane I have grown but rather how much more insane I have been prevented from becoming.

At least they try, I'll give them that, my earnest and smiling jailers. But I am unforgivable.

My father was completely mad, but he was craftier than I. He never killed anyone, which is how they always catch you, but he wanted to, especially himself. My father taught me the two essentials for living successfully while insane: lie quickly and often, and believe in as many different and contradictory ideas at once as you can. The golden misrules.

When I was about eleven years old, one of the men who worked with my father, I forget his name now, took a keen interest in me and my many and changing emotional states. *Don't be sad, come sit on my lap. Don't be afraid, come sit on my lap. Don't act like a sissy, come sit on my lap. Don't*, he told me in dozens of different ways, *be the child you are, and please come and sit on my lap.* His seduction technique was simple: he noticed that I was feeling one way, and he knew that I, like any boy on the verge of puberty, was never certain what I should feel, and he would propose that I feel the opposite way instead. Bait and switch. On his lap. I was remarkably gullible, especially for a smart-mouthed brat.

I do remember that the man – what was his name? – was singularly ugly, cartoonishly ugly, a male hag. His face was covered in polyps, brown and oily skin tags in various states of maturity; some hung off his face and swung like pendulums when he laughed, some were new growths, barely more than moles, some were hard, fingernail-hard, some were fatty globules. I know this because he encouraged me to touch them. *Don't be afraid*, he said, *don't be afraid. It's only skin.* And then he would kiss me, on the lips, down my neck. I have a half memory of him cupping my behind, at first playfully, pretending to spank me, and then more slowly, his fingers lingering on the curve of my ass. A half memory – I cannot swear he did this. How much do I really want to know about the past? If he did molest me, expose himself, or have me perform sex acts with him, I don't remember the events. My testimony would not hold up in court.

But I remember how he smelled. Of gasoline and wax. He worked in a garage, pumping gas and washing windows and changing oil. He always wore the same overalls, light blue zip-up overalls smeared with petroleum. And he smoked, Player's Light. How did he not burst into flame? I remember that he lived with his mother, and that his mother cut his hair and combed it for him every morning. He told me that much himself. *It's okay if you love somebody*, he told me, *okay to touch and fuss and tickle. Let me comb your hair. Do you feel better now? Oh, not another tear! Now, let me catch it in my mouth, for good luck.*

The gas man and I had quite the affair. Even my older brother noticed it, and he barely recognized me most of the time. I think now that it must have been my brother who broke up my first romance. I will never have the chance to thank him. Or blame him. What would he do with either, with gratitude or accusations, messages from the forgotten brother, the brother in the cage, my foggy ideas of the past, a time that is nothing but clean and clear.

My brother blabbed, my father reacted, and my first love got a new job in another town. My father took me for a long walk along the stone beach beside our house. He made me sit down on a driftwood branch that was covered in sand and sea salt, broken strips of kelp. I remember that I was wearing white pants and I didn't want to get them dirty because in an hour I would be seeing my best friend, and he would kiss me and sit me down on his knee and tell me a dirty joke that I would pretend to understand. But not if my pants were dirty. I was a good boy, I was a good boy. I was not a dirty boy. I was not.

You think Mr. (what was his name, damn me) loves you, my father started off, *but he does not. He loves you in a way that is not right. It feels right to you because you don't understand. He loves you in a way he thinks is right and you think is right but that everybody else knows is wrong. He lies to you. When he says he loves you he is telling the truth to himself, but the truth is different for him because he is not right in the head. Everyone is talking about what you do with him and you are embarrassing me. Don't tell anyone. You are too big to be sitting on a man's knee. Stop crying or I'll turn you over my knee and then you'll have a reason to cry. It's all right for grown-ups to touch and tickle each other but not for two men. I don't want you ruined. You are enough of a heartbreak to me now. It's not your fault. Why did you keep going back to him after the first time? Your brother is ashamed of you. Come home now to your family who loves you.*

And that was my first informed introduction to madness. Fact and counter-fact. All statements have an opposite. Everything is true, especially whatever you don't understand. You are to blame for all the good and all the bad in your own life, and never forget the world is full of bad people who want to hurt you. I love you, but I will hit you. There is no such thing as a good secret, now stop making a spectacle of yourself. Love is unconditional, until there are problems.

My father stood as far away as he could from me, me and the grimy driftwood, us dirty things. He had to almost yell, but of course he could not yell out all that terrible information. We were alone, alone on a cold pebble beach, alone on a windy day, a day that howled, with the tides booming all around us, a good day to be deaf, and his first concern was that no one overheard him, that only I heard the real message buried in his rambling speech: *You are as mad as me. You can live with wrong and right together too. You will be watched from now on. I hate you because you can love. I will teach you to distrust yourself.*

My father led me home, me in front, him in the back, looking around. *Stop slouching*, he said. *People will think I beat you. People will think you live in a bad home. Nobody likes a hunchback.*

My brother was gone, packed off to our grandparents for a week. My mother was frantically cleaning my room, rubbing the carpet to raw threads with the vacuum. I could smell vinegar – she'd cleaned my window, inside and out. She'd gone through my bookshelf, throwing anything that was not a book into the trash: the bright red leaves I pressed between wax sheets, the blobs of beach glass, the dried black kelp seed pods that smelled of iodine. *They'll go mouldy*, she said. *And I washed your rock collection*, she said. *Stop bringing things home.*

My father went to his study and closed the door. I could hear his television, the old black-and-white set he kept for his own use. He watched an old cowboy film. He loved cowboy movies. The house was full of the sounds of gunshots and complaining livestock, a language of men. I was full of hate.

When my psychiatrists ask me if I had a good relationship with my father, I smile. *Oh, yes*, I say. *We were peas in a pod. We did everything together. I am his copy.* I was certain when I was a boy that Daddy could read my mind.

My third meeting with Alexandar became our first date. What an odd word: *date*. What had we been doing before?

I was drinking at Turandot on Bergmanstrasse, another pre-unification relic, but without the petty thieves, cops, or joyfully bad music. Turandot was a punk bar for nice people with jobs. Underneath the glaze created by decades of uninterrupted (and never wiped off) tobacco smoke and cheap candle wax, masses of iron wrought to resemble tree roots covered the walls and ceiling. From the main root that hovered over the bar, dozens of thin, curly tendrils peeled downward, ending in forks, devils' tails, crammed with green candles.

'You're a little tall to be a hobbit.'

Alexandar, again. Unlikely as always, belly to the bar. I stared, tried not to blink.

'This bar, Martin – it's like being underground. In a hobbit hole.'

'Yes, I got that.'

'Of course. I forgot. You are the clever one.'

'I never know if *clever* is a compliment or not.'

Alexandar gave my right earlobe a hard tug and led me to a table. 'Now,' he said, 'now you will tell me why you ran away from home.'

When someone you barely know asks you an intimate question, lie. I told Alexandar I was a person too easily calmed, a person so faintly aware of my surroundings and the anxieties of others that I sought out the remote, the other, the new and alienating, just to keep going. I told Alexandar I realized, at forty-seven, that I was not complicated enough. I told Alexandar

I had gone with the flow for years, too long, until I realized I was in truth being washed over, not propelled forward. I used every psychosocial term I could remember from decades of therapy, but in reverse. A man needs to be active, no? A man needs to contribute, not just watch, no?

Alexandar nodded, spellbound by the ineptness of my lies. A dog would have smelled my lies.

But once I started to tell Alexandar how I had cleaned out my home in Toronto, thrown away everything I owned until there was nothing left but the clothes in my suitcase and a handful of trinkets in a makeup bag, charms and a crystal pendant and a photograph of my mother and an oily black stone from a beach in Iceland, he began to really listen. He leaned into my body, pressing me for more, for a story.

'How many things?' he asked. 'What kinds of things? Truly, and books too? And paintings and furniture? But no one does this,' he said. 'No one who can imagine the future. No adult.'

'I started from the bottom,' I told him, 'and worked my way up. The obvious junk went fast.'

'And what is junk?' he asked.

'North American things,' I told him. 'Ornaments and Christmas lights, stockpiles of incense, crime novels, fading houseplants, a Blue Willow dinner service for twenty-four, anything kept because of the memories it triggered, not because it was useful.'

'Germans,' Alexandar boasted, 'do not keep for the sake of keeping.'

And how can they afford to, I thought, *if they want to live outside history?* But I said nothing.

'And next,' Alexandar asked, nudging me in the shoulder. 'Next you destroyed what?'

'No, not destroyed, removed.' Alexandar pulled a face. 'I gave my things away,' I said.

'Ah,' he nodded. 'Like a saint. And did you eat dirt too?'

And how you would love to watch that, Alexandar, I whispered to myself, *how you would enjoy me on the ground in front of you, at your boots, licking mud off my fingers.*

I cleared my throat. 'The furniture went next,' I continued. 'Furniture is the easiest thing in the world to be rid of. What more do you need but a bed, a chair, and a table? One lamp. One cup, one plate, one spoon, and one knife. One of one, that was the rule. The paintings? Most art is better off in a sealed box. How do you tell a friend that, in truth, you do not love him? Give him your art. And people who keep books they have already read are merely insecure. There is a difference between knowing who you are and being your own librarian, a dusty archivist who lives in constant fear of fire. Books are not objects, they are vehicles. There is nothing sadder than a shelf full of unmolested literature. I should know, I've created enough of the stuff myself.'

'You are a man of ideas,' Alexandar laughed as he playfully slapped me on the back of the head, hinting at more to come. 'A man of ideas, and a man who does not believe in leaving evidence! Can the two men live together? Do you chase yourself around with a blade, around your bare table, like the wolf against his tail? This is a story for children! Stop now. I might take you at your face.'

We left the bar and walked straight to my apartment. We made love in my bed. Alexandar came inside me with a sigh and then fell asleep. I got up and made a drink. I read a crime novel. An hour later, Alexandar sat down beside me on the couch and laced up his boots.

'That was nice,' I said. 'I'm an idiot.'

'Yes, nice. So very nice. We are nice men.' Alexandar grinned. He zipped his bomber jacket all the way up to his neck and jerked back his head, looking at my apartment and all the new things I had already bought for it, all the decorating, the way I made a space my own with colourful objects.

'Yes, a nice night out,' he said. 'Nice boys like nice things, don't we?'

He kissed me hard. I felt his teeth on my tongue, his spit shot down my throat. I began to pull back, but he caught the back of my head between his forearm and bicep. His saliva trickled out of my mouth and down my chin. I remember that it burned, just a little, like eucalyptus balm, laundry detergent, the red end of a spent match. He broke away from me, stood up straight, and was at the door in two steps.

'Now you know,' he said. 'My new little friend, he sees me. I can lie too.'

I consulted the Tarot, a three-card spread. Who is this man who knows me and all my tricks but has never spoken my full name?

The King of Cups. The Chariot. The Four of Pentacles. Excess, conquest, equilibrium. How perfect.

The King of Cups is, of course, a man. The rider of the Chariot is a man. The King of Cups faces the reader in near profile, with his head turned slightly to the left, to the sinister. The rider of the Chariot stares forward, his expression neither cold nor hot, aggressive nor passive.

The King of Cups sits on a high-backed throne decorated with two dancing fish, fish rising up from the surface of the water, rampant (the symbol of Pisces, my birth sign). The rider of the Chariot stands on a dais. His chariot has no wheels. A canopy frames him, decorated in rich fabric dotted with Stars of David. Behind the canopy, a city waits. Is he the guard or the conqueror?

The Chariot is pulled by two Sphinxes, one black, one white. They sit, cherub-faced, calm as murderers. The King of Cups appears to be raising one eyebrow, doubtful, or watchful, or amused. Both men are crowned, but who truly rules?

Both men are still: the King seated, resplendent in a shoulder-to-ground robe, a robe as opaque and unyielding as any iron gate, and the rider, elevated and armed with a staff, standing guard over his monsters, a pagan Aaron. The King's throne sits atop a small mound of rocky ground, surrounded by rippling water. He reigns over a river, or a lake, perhaps the shallows of an ocean. The rider's Chariot is parked on speckled sand. All beneath me, the rider tells us, is dust.

Opposites and counterpoints. Sand and water, movement and stasis, the city and the ocean, the rider's brilliant armour and the King's plush robes. Were they real men, two nobles, how they would hate each other, and rightly so. One must be the master of the other. So nature dictates. But nature is never of one mind. Nature breaks her toys.

The Four of Pentacles annoyed me. It was only an echo. Four is a square, four is an equal, four is two twos, double symmetry. Four Pentacles. Pentacles are meant to represent money. A Pentacle sits inside a double-lined circle. It is a coin. *What's that got to do with me*, I wondered. I had enough money to last. I lived carefully, I watched my bottom line.

But there are other kinds of currencies. Coins of this realm, yes, the exact and extraordinary sums needed to build a life, monies to which I could never afford to be oblivious and am still not, and then the tolls paid in less tangible rarities, the kinds not pressed in copper or gold. Costs in spirit, in health, the ten thousand little fines we pay for our confidence, for our learning and cultivating, for acquiring tastes and playing the game, the damned game, of making and making and making more. Even fools have expenses.

The Four of Pentacles, I told myself, I can pay that much. For Alexandar, the King of Cups, the cloaked man flush with fine drink, the man on the island, the stony island with just enough room for his throne, and me. I will pay in cum and repartee, a few shared meals, gruff pleasantries. *He's only a man, I told myself, and what do men need? Distraction and release, rough novelties. I did not pull my whole life up out of the ground, shake the dirt off the roots and cut into fresh earth, cross an ocean, just to be lazy, to fail to thrive. Alexandar is my Berlin project. I know now why I am here. He's only a man.*

I scooped up the cards and shuffled the King, the rider, and the Four back into the deck. I wrapped the deck up in fresh wax paper and hid it in the armoire, behind a stack of clean, paired socks. *I don't want him stumbling on my idiosyncrasies before we've even spent a whole night in each other's arms,* I thought, *before we have slept in the same bed and gotten used to the sounds we make, before we have been unconscious together. Before he trusts me.*

I made myself a cup of tea and watched the early-morning traffic plod past my front window. *How lumpy these people are,* I said to myself, forgetting that I was wearing dirty pyjamas and smelled like Alexandar's armpits, how overdressed and clumsy. Love is not blind, it just can't see itself in a mirror. Love is a lower form of mammal.

I drained the cup and, out of habit, glanced at the leaves. There were no shapes, no patterns, no arrows, hearts, rings, flowers, birds in flight. The leaves sat in a conical mound in the centre of the cup, a tiny mountain in a tiny valley. And I stupidly told myself I was looking at a tower, not a bullet.

All throughout my first few months in Berlin, I had a nagging sense that I was missing something. Not an actual object, a tool or a comfort I had forgotten to pack along with me, and not the unspecific longing that is homesickness, but a feeling that Berlin itself was incomplete, that a vital flavour was absent from the city's otherwise perfect, and perfectly contradictory, mixture of melancholy and jolliness, remembrance and wilful forgetting.

And then it dawned on me, entirely by accident. I was wandering around the packed Sunday flea market in Mauerpark – a tawdry, gorgeous mess of exotic antiques and awful hippie crafts, pricey and neatly presented high-end retail rejigged for the outdoors and buckets of ten-euro-cents-apiece plastic toys, professional junk dealers and broke students selling off their old clothes and half-burned candles. I came upon a stall selling mass-produced patches, badges, tote bags, and T-shirts, all covered in images of ancient rock bands and their album covers. Led Zeppelin, Iron Maiden, Boston, Queen, the Who, a limitless supply of Beatles heralds. The customers swarming the kiosk were all speaking English: Brits and Americans and Australians. This is what was missing, I realized. Berlin is not clotted with boomer nostalgia.

Growing up in North America, I could never escape the 1960s and their supposed glories. I had naturalized the idea that the music and imagery from that decade, and whatever was achieved by the people who were young during that time, represented a pinnacle in world culture. I knew this was a lie, but knowing water drowns and surviving a flood are two different things.

Berlin has no 'oldies' radio stations, no classic-rock tribute bars, no Woodstock memorabilia stores. Even the closely watched bong-and-rolling-papers shops sell posters of Tupac, Lil' Kim, and Al Pacino in *Scarface*, not pictures of John Lennon or the undead billionaires who run Rolling Stones Inc. Bumper stickers bearing the Hand of Fatima are more common than glue-backed peace signs.

Berliners cannot be both nostalgic and contrite. And they must always be contrite. Nostalgia leads to morbidity, or worse, a wilful, forced forgetting, the collective equivalent of leaving your troubles at the bottom of a bottle. Berliners must pay, and pay, and pay. No one living here can ignore the simple truth that everything around them, from airports to apartment towers, dignified bars with polished brass beer pumps to seniors' homes, department stores to mucky canals, was built with blood, torture, murder, and rage. Nostalgia is not a cozy blanket in Berlin, it is a sizzling fuse. Reach for it at your peril.

Good, I thought. *Good for them. Berliners have escaped the boomer plague. For all the wrong reasons, but that is not my problem to solve. I can live here in full confidence that days and weeks will pass between accidental brushes with 'Hey Jude' or 'My Generation,' the maudlin, limp-cock stroking of the Doors, Joni Mitchell's fucking parking lot. To live in a culture free of self-congratulation is a kind of miracle, a blessing. You can't pat yourself on the back in Berlin for things you never did, and no politician is ever photographed playing guitar with Sir Paul McCartney.*

For a professional contrarian, which is what I was, Berlin was a challenge. There was no über-generation to blame for the ruination of the planet, the economy, my youth. I faced a stark choice: find new things to be against – impossible in a place where I understood not one word of the language or any of the simple indulgences that are the bedrock of a culture, the food and drink, how handshakes are performed, what to wear in nice restaurants, how clothes are sized – or simply learn to love. Learn to be loved.

I loved Alexandar with confidence, a belief in myself that bordered on egomania, and one that quickly devolved into gluttony. I felt I could take all that he offered and give him back twice as much. For the first time in my life, my experiences were not second-hand, were not cloaked in a previous culture's triumphalism, were not gauged beside a set of standards I had no part in establishing, a musty paisley cloak pulled over my head. I wanted to inhale Alexandar – his body, his mind, his words, his actions, calm or violent. My history was valid, my experiences worth sharing. I was not an echo, an X, a bust after a boom, a man living between important times.

I felt so free. I had a few years of youth left to spend, a body ready, flawed but able, I had no debts but I was owed plenty: late nights and foolish talk, long careless fuckings and dreamy talk under blankets, afternoons to waste, tickling and pinching, rooms lit by one hundred candles, alleys reeking with cat piss and unwashed ass, glamour, pointless arguments, bondage games that took hours to play, panic attacks and patience, new shoes, new friends, being the bottom or being the top, or both, more kisses than a wedding procession, Alexandar's tongue, rough as an old belt, deep in my throat, to be smothered until the world went black. I would take up smoking. I would eat meat again. I would shoplift and be a cunt to bank clerks. I would look down at the cobbles and seek out dog shit to step on, to grind into my heels. I'd fart on the U-Bahn.

Only by being whatever I was not before, by killing Canadian Martin, could I catch and hold Alexandar. Canadian Martin measured himself in tons. Berlin Martin's pockets were empty.

Berlin Martin levitated at will. Berlin Martin was always wet between his legs, ready. Berlin Martin ate his own pre-cum and tasted cloves, sesame seeds, fresh-cut hay. Berlin Martin would die with his boots off, tied around his neck.

In Germany, pigs are symbols of good luck and prosperity. It is hardly an insult to send a friend a picture of a pig and wish him a happy birthday, or a long-wedded life, or a pleasant voyage. Berlin Martin became a wild boar, bristled and always hungry. Berlin Martin found gold in mud. Berlin Martin was the luckiest creature that ever grew tusks and a corkscrew tail. Pigs are always happy, and then they are eaten.

'That's a ridiculous way to live.' Alexandar stood over me at Turandot, digging in his pockets for his phone, his cigarettes, his lighter. He was forever misplacing small things.

'Which way? I live at least four different ways at once. Like most people.'

'This idea about the people in the 1960s controlling your life. You can control your life.'

'Until you've heard Country Joe & the Fish at Woodstock forty thousand times, you can't comment.'

'No, no. Clever will not do here. I am taking it for serious. The past is dead, you are alive.'

'I'm not arguing that I am any less alive, only that this is the first place I have ever lived where the accomplishments of the previous generation have not been celebrated constantly, to the point where I feel like my own life and accomplishments are not genuine, are not worth doing or noticing or – '

'Stop there. Noticing by who?'

'Me.'

'So, you are making this rule for yourself against yourself.'

'No,' I sighed. 'This is how it works in North America: one generation – the boomers we call them – run everything. There is youth culture, yes, but it all reflects back on the boomer culture. And there is a culture that my generation, the half generation, made and still make, but nobody cares about it. In Canada, I feel invisible. In Berlin, I think there is a chance for me, maybe my last chance because I am older now, I am not young, to be completely self-actualized – '

'The words you have!'

'Completely certain that whatever I do next is important. Big important, small important, that doesn't matter – what matters is that there is no big cloud of dead culture hanging over me and telling me that I will never have any sunshine – '

'In Berlin? No big dark clouds?' Alexandar found his cigarettes and sat down. He pushed the ashtray to the far end of the table. So considerate. 'Everyone is an island. A little island. That English poem is a lie. But also islands are under the sun and the rain and all that. So, we are all together also. Everyone alone and everyone together. People who are crazy can't be both – they have to be all alone or all with all the other people, and then there is a kind of mania. You are not crazy, you are just stupid-smart. You think everything out and notice nothing. Maybe you know some bad times in your past, and maybe there is a good reason to say "this is because of those older people" – I am German, I understand that thought better than you. All my life and it will not stop for maybe one hundred more years. But there is also the idea of now. Has it ever been in your head that these boombers – '

'Boomers.'

'Yes, okay. Booo-mers. Maybe they are living under a curse?'

'If having everything is a curse, yes.'

Alexandar lifted his hands up in surrender. 'I think also you will make me the crazy person.'

'I'm doing the best I can.'

'Okay, let me say it this way: you, Martin, Mr. Martin, you are telling me you are happy. It's correct?'

'Happy, but – '

'No. Stop.'

'Happy. Yes.'

'Now you must say nothing else. What we do here is for us.'

'You Germans have so many polite ways of telling people to shut up.'

'Oh, and tricks too!' Alexandar kissed me. His mouth tasted of cardamom and beer bubbles. We walked back to my apartment as fast as we could. Alexandar stayed one step behind me, tugging at the belt loops in my sagging jeans. Step, tug. Step, tug. A pony game. Obedience training.

Before I had a moment to lock my front door, I was bent over the loveseat in my living room. My pants were unbuttoned and pulled down in four seconds. I heard Alexandar unzip and then felt him inside me. His cock was thick at the top, thick as an elbow. I bit the collar of my T-shirt, remembered to breathe. *So fast*, I thought, *I am never open so fast*. I take forever. I am too tightly wound, inside and out. Alexandar's legs rubbed against the tops of my thighs. He was wearing wool pants. The fabric tickled, then warmed. I felt all the blood and water in my body pool in my stomach. My fingertips and toes were numb. My head spun. I came in two hard jolts. My cum was runny and yellowy white, the colour of a spoiled egg. I don't know if Alexandar came inside me or not.

I poured caraway schnapps into two tall glasses. Alexandar sat on my couch, pleased with himself. *If I had a library here*, I thought, *he'd walk around it pulling out books, inspecting my tastes, and he would nod or tsk-tsk. He would walk the room with his hands behind his back, like a curious soldier. There would be questions.* But I had no library. Only rented furniture and trinkets, a space heater and a lamp, a collapsible daybed.

I sat beside him and he gently turned me sideways and pulled my feet up onto his lap. He peeled off my socks and pressed his thumb into my left arch. My ears popped.

'Do that again,' I said, and he did. 'A philosopher and a reflexologist. I'm a lucky boy.'

Alexandar covered my right foot with both his hands. He locked his fingers together and squeezed. I felt sleepy. The back of my neck began to sweat. I gulped the schnapps.

Someone two floors above us decided to take a hot shower. Every piece of metal behind the walls and ceiling screamed into action. I'd become used to the civil war between the water and the pipes. Alexandar sat, stunned and goggle-eyed, waiting for the roof to fall in. He finished his schnapps in one swallow.

'Someday if you are good, I will tell you the story of the Viy.'

I was never faithful to Alexandar, not at first and not at the last. I disliked the very word *faithful*. It was ridiculous. Alexandar and I were not practising a religious ritual, had not sworn a holy oath. Monogamy is not natural to me, it is an imposition.

I hardly expected Alexandar to have sex only with me, even after we began to see each other almost daily. I expected him to have a normal, healthy gay sex drive, a need for variety. And neither of us was living in a rural village, without options or opportunities, without other horses in other barns. Berlin is a glutton's heaven, whatever your needs are – liquor, drugs, art, sex, protracted conversation, towering cakes. Lust and banking are the city's primary industries.

Nevertheless, I slowed down, stopped cruising every night. The fall bore down on me, made me sleepy.

Autumn in Berlin is not crisp, not new-apple shiny. Autumn in Berlin does not prompt the mind to think of new beginnings, 'the social season,' of cleaning up one's act and getting down to work. Autumn in Berlin is dark and wet. The sun falls out of the sky promptly at 3:30 p.m. There is no half-light hour. Rain arrives first in the early morning, then again at 9:00 or 10:00 p.m., just when you're all dressed up for a party. The rain is cold and oily and sprays the streets unevenly. The rain never falls straight down, so an umbrella is useless. The wet cobbles defeat hiking boots, walking canes, and heavy carts. Berliners are forever skinning their knees and elbows on slick pavement.

And when the sun comes out, resentfully, once a week, or, stranger still, stays out, well into 4:00 or even 5:00 p.m., everyone drops what they are doing to sit under the still green and leafy trees, or to jockey and bicker for a prime sidewalk café seat, one facing outward, the better to judge and giggle at passersby.

The trees do not change colour. There is no fall show of flaming leaves. The leaves are green, then paler green, and then are not there at all. Only the horse chestnuts bother to drop their fuzzy seed balls and clutter the sidewalks with enormous, tangerine, trident-shaped leaves, to acknowledge the change of season. Children collect the seed balls, peel them open and spear the soft nuts with toothpicks, glue on googly eyes, making chestnut men, chestnut cows, towers, cars, and elaborate chestnut castles that take up entire windowsills.

Fall is so slow to come in Berlin, and so dull, that stores sell baskets overflowing with fake orange leaves and fake acorns, plastic squirrels hoarding plastic nuts, 'winter flavour' tea and 'winter odour' soap (both of which smell of cranberries, burnt logs, and dry red wine). After all, there is nature in Berlin, and then there is the market reality. Berliners want their seasonal symbols when they want them, not whenever they might arrive. Berliners are chronically impatient and fantastically stubborn. If the date is October 1, a Berliner will wear a winter scarf and hat and coat even if the temperature outside is twenty degrees, because those are the clothes you wear in October, and the calendar trumps the thermometer.

And so, in October, I followed the local example: I fucked for warmth, as if my extremities were in danger of frostbite. I had yet to turn the heat on in my apartment, and I slept with my windows open, but I went after physical contact with a resigned desperation, like a mountaineer stuck on a snowy ledge who cuddles with his sherpas and sled dogs for their body heat.

If we are all pretending the earth is frozen over and the trees are bare, I thought, *I want the benefits: the rough, sweaty fucking that goes on under quilts in mid-winter, the saving-heating-costs.*

The least confusing aspect of living in Berlin was my relationship to other artists. It was exactly the same as the take-and-take relationship I had with creative people in Toronto. I was a conduit to the magic world of 'press,' nothing more.

Whatever I made or wanted to make, did or wanted to do, was amusing at best, but irrelevant. I was a tool, a device, forgotten as soon as the job was done, a cold hammer dropped on a table. I had no larger identity for them, and before long I began to believe myself to be as empty of talent and value as they made me feel. A convenient idiot. The fat man from the newspaper.

The Canadians were the worst. I predicted as much before I left Toronto. The great difference, one I admit I found admirable for being so bald and so shameless, was that the Canadian artists who thought I might do their careers some good openly told me as much and made sure I was invited to all their events.

A photo shoot here, a gallery vernissage there. The first night (with free drinks until 8:00 p.m.!) of a new lounge-cum-gallery-cum-barbershop-cum-performance space. A live DJ set. A panel discussion on 'process and practice.' A new dance work set to noises made by the buses that run from Tel Aviv to Ramallah, a collection of neo-primitive paintings made by an artist in his twenties who had never heard of neo-primitivism. A first night at a bespoke shoe shop, a first night at a tattoo parlour, a first night at a spa specializing in hot-pepper rubs. Three terrible art exhibitions held in the back of vintage clothing stores, exhibitions completely defeated by the enormous fifties ball gowns and spectacular seventies platform shoes on offer. A sixtieth birthday party for a curator, one who had turned down my own work half a dozen times in the past. Could I come early, could I bring my own camera and recorder? The curator has an exciting new venture to announce …

The art world is bitter and hateful, from Berlin to Beirut to Bobcaygeon. I accepted every invitation, because so am I. The possibility that a fellow Canadian would fail in Berlin, fail spectacularly, was too entrancing to resist. One needs something to write home about. I bought an expensive tube of tooth-whitening paste. My smile was a snowdrift, clean and bright and unstable.

Artists all want the same thing, me included. They want an antidote. The world is large and full of colour and noise. The vibrancy of the world is poison to artists. We want to be larger, contain more colours, be louder. But we can't. We're defeated before we start. Put any ten people from any walk of life in front of Picasso's *Guernica* or one of Pollock's monstrous swirls and they will stare, perhaps even cry. But if a cute puppy suddenly wanders into the room, the masterpiece disappears. All art is ultimately inanimate, and the human mind seeks out and prizes things that twitch and twinkle, roar and stink – the hummingbird is mightier than the cathedral. This is not to put so-called nature above art, but to merely recognize that an active stimulus will always be more seductive than an inactive distraction. For artists, the cure is to become the distraction themselves, to become the watched object. To be the beloved, not the lover, the puppy, not the Pollock.

I understood exactly what was expected of me. Nod and smile, nod and smile. Ask a considered question, ask another. Watch the art, but more importantly the artist, like a soldier watching a gate, be on the lookout for sudden movement, noises offstage, sudden drops in temperature, an eerie stillness. I understood my role, and I hated myself for being so adaptable. I could no more decline the pile of invitations than I could decline to breathe. I was part of the system, I made artists, the makers, into attractions, into objects of desire, and I did it very well. I was rewarded with more calls for my presence, my attendance, and so had become an attraction myself. Codependency travels well.

I brought Alexandar to a handful of opening nights, but after the fifth or sixth he refused to attend any more.

'These people are not your friends,' he told me, quietly, flat-voiced, the way you might tell someone that their mother had died or that they were becoming an alcoholic.

'Friends?' I asked him. 'Friends? All those people you met? We're just sharing needles.'

Alexandar pulled a long face. It was almost comical. 'There is a large difference when power games are for sex and when power games are how you make a life.'

'How large?'

'In the first you play evil, in the second you do evil.'

How do you tell the man you love that you love him the most when you think he's going to kill you?

To the City of Thieves!

Alexandar and I were getting drunk at Franken with B and K, two painters from Toronto. Alexandar held forth on all things Berlin, sublime and silly. He was shouting and proposing toast after toast, as loud and puppy-clumsy as any beer-hall lout. My big man, my sweet and foolish big man.

I'd never seen Alexandar so boisterous or heard him talk so much. I was proud of my handsome new fellow, and I wanted to show him off to my fellow expats, guys I trusted to report the news of Martin's Berlin Boyfriend back to Toronto, back to my old circles and their itching, jealous ears. Gossips are trustworthy people, in their fashion. And painters live for cheap talk.

'Certainly you have noticed,' Alexandar began again, looking around the table like a professor instructing his top pupils, his pets, 'everything has two prices: the German price and the Ausländer price?'

'Berlin has a madness: money. In the back of every German's mind there is a grandmother's stories of no food, no heat, no shoes, cold hands, cold streets, no wool, broken windows, no coal. Berlin is the worst. I tell you, the richest man in Berlin believes, truly, all his life can go up and then down – How do you say it? Like this?'

Alexandar put his right hand over his left, then quickly put the left over the right.

'Topsy-turvy,' K said.

'Yes, so! Toopsah-turkey. And then his life is over! I say it is a mania for Berliners. Disaster is hanging in the sky and sleeping in the water, always. So Berliners, they scratch, like rats, scratch scratch scratch for one euro here and two euros there, and they watch for luck – Oh! Here is my chance to make fifty cents! I will cheat this man! For fifty cents! Now I have held up the sky for a little longer. It is like madness but more exhausting. This is why all the people you see on the trains are half-asleep – they are tired from fear and from cutting each other all day. And when they hear you speaking your English, their grand-mother's voice inside the brains says: "That is an American! He is rich! You can get twenty cents more from him, you can get a whole euro. Americans own the moon itself. Quick, quick, ask him for the moon!"'

'So, you're going to stiff us for the drinks?' B asked.

'Ha! No!' Alexandar slapped B on the back and shook me by the shoulders. 'Only this one! Martin I will take to his house and stiff good, maybe when he is asleep.' Alexandar slapped B on the back again, harder.

K looked at me and smiled. *I don't care if I spend all day tomorrow throwing up,* I thought, *that look was worth it. In twelve hours half of Toronto will know that ugly stupid old Martin is getting fucked by a hot German.*

'I do not consider money,' Alexandar carried on. 'My grand-mother has been dead for thirty years. She never talked much and nobody asked her questions. And so I steal the money I need. Not so much, only what I must have. I am a prince in the City of Thieves.'

'Bullshit.' K grinned at Alexandar, in that half-aggressive, half-gleeful way men challenge each other about what is true and what is not. A good lie, the grin says, is forgivable if it's worth hearing.

'I will not tell all my secrets but I say I am a prince. What does a prince do? He helps his king, he is good to his queen. I know many kings in Berlin. I am helpful. Russian kings, Serbian kings, Greek kings – many, many Greek kings. A few Spanish ones too. Let you imagine that there is a box. Inside the box could be anything at all. You must not care.

'A king needs to take the box from here – ' Alexandar dipped his fingers into a pool of spilled beer and drew a wet line across the table' – to over here. But he cannot do this, he is the king. People know him. His German is not so super. His hair is very black and his shoes are too shiny. He is only almost a German. But a real German, a nice German man in simple clothes? A white man? I am just like the river water. I flow past.'

'You're a mule,' B said, fascinated.

'How is that word?'

'Mule. A donkey. It's what we say in English when you deliver things for somebody else. He is my mule.'

Alexandar roared with laughter. He banged his fists on the table. The waitress arrived immediately. He spoke to her in German. She laughed and went back to the bar to fetch us fresh drinks.

'I am a donkey! I have to tell this word to my kings. I hope they do not decide to beat their poor donkey with a stick. Poor donkey!'

B looked a little ashamed of himself. 'I'm sorry,' he started, but Alexandar gave him a reassuring clip on the back of the head.

'No, no. We are all relaxing. Friends with friends. And now I am like your Indians. I have my man name and my animal name.'

B and K drank up quickly. B checked his phone. K said something about an important studio visit the next day, about a curator from Vienna. In ten minutes, Alexandar and I were crossing Oranienstrasse in the cold fog. Alexandar walked behind me. He pretended to fix the knot in my scarf, straighten my collar, but really he just wanted to cop a feel, get underneath my coat. I felt a warmth on my back, fingers counting my vertebrae.

'I like your friends, Martin. I like painters. Why are all of your friends artists?'

'Bad luck.'

We walked to my apartment arm in arm. Alexandar was quiet. I worried that he was upset. We arrived and I unlocked the door to my lobby. The lights were burnt-out and the lobby was dark, dark and cold. I unlocked my apartment door and turned to Alexandar. He was standing in the middle of the lobby unzipping his pants.

I went to him. He pushed me to my knees. I could feel the cold tiles through my jeans. I panicked. What if somebody came home? Alexandar held the back of my head. He was not erect. I bent toward him, my mouth open. A hot stream of urine splashed on my face, scalding, electric. I gasped, tried to jump back, but Alexandar's grip was firm, eager, digging. He pissed on my face until it was soaked and finished up with a last spurt down the front of my coat. I knelt in the warm pool, stupid and stunned and wet. He zipped up.

'Up, up. Come on.' Alexandar gently lifted me off the lobby floor, his hands under my armpits. 'You can do it. Up now. Don't worry about the piss. Isn't this building full of wild children?'

Inside, Alexandar walked me to the bathroom and peeled off my clothes, throwing everything into the tub. He left his piss to drip off my face and hair. The piss smelled like apples. I didn't resist. My apartment was warm and humid and I was drunk and disoriented and hard. Alexandar undressed and we curled into bed. He covered our bodies with a fuzzy blanket. He took my cock between his thumb and forefinger and jerked the foreskin until I came. I kicked and tensed as cum streamed out of me in three long, stringy shots. Alexandar put his legs on top of mine, pinned me down. I don't think I have ever been happier. Or ever will be so happy again.

Alexandar tucked the blanket tight under my body and covered me with his arms and legs. He dug his chin into my neck. His breath was cold. Strangely cold. I felt his chest hair warming my shoulders, but his breath was making the back of my head numb. Alcohol has always had unpredictable effects on my senses.

'The Viy,' Alexandar whispered, 'knows the true name of the Devil.'

The Viy is not a demon. Demons are common, and plentiful. The Viy is singular, is part of no hierarchy, is not a mock angel.

The Viy is not a monster. Monsters live inside bodies, as we understand the constitution of 'a body.' The Viy is intangible but bears a form, is material and yet not subject to material laws. You cannot kill the Viy with silver, stakes, atomic weapons, the Holy Ghost, fresh water. The Viy lives by its own laws.

The Viy is known to the Devil and perhaps was once the Devil's lover. This question is hotly disputed. The Viy operates in concert with the Devil but is not ruled by him. The Viy is older, by uncountable numbers of centuries, than the Devil.

The Viy was born of the earth itself. The Viy is older than evil and never aspired to good, or to greatness. If the Devil is the Fallen One, the Viy is one who never rose. The Viy is. To question the Viy's origins is to question the birth of dust, the genealogy of mud. We can only know the Viy by its works.

There are no reliable creation myths, no formative histories, no heroisms or misdeeds to recount. The Viy is outside of chronicles, tales, all narratives. By comparison, the Devil is himself only a long, tangled story. The Viy is tongue and teeth and breath and spit. The Devil is merely the words that came so much later. The Devil is a song, the Viy is the notes, guttural or sweet, and especially the broken chords.

But the Viy leaves traces. The Viy can be tracked. We were not made with senses for no reason. The Viy is not all-powerful. How could mud and ore be?

As we are born with touch and taste, so was the Viy bred of sensation and muck. As we are animals that feel and from feeling know, the Viy is the antithesis; the Viy is present, always, and reality bends around it. This is our one advantage, that the Viy is not of nature. Not of our nature. We are clever sensualists, we recognize difference, apartness, interruptions. If we were also immortal, the Viy would be as invisible and yet acknowledged by our senses, as known and understood (and perhaps as ignored) as air, as light.

But we can find the Viy only when it prances to the rhythms of animal time, when it bothers to be known to us, for its own amusement. Alarms go off, ears prick up. Particles charge. Noses itch. Something wicked this way, etc. Heads ring and cheeks flush.

The Viy is a fever is a fugue is a dizzy spell is indigestion is the gag reflex is a rash a sore a canker is a suspicion is a blackout is a dry mouth is bloating is apnea is heart failure is a dilated pupil is a racing pulse. The Viy is a symptom. At first. The Viy is indirection, disorder incarnate. Not chaos, chaos is too grand. The Viy is a pest, uncommon. No one has perfected a trap.

Here is what is known of the Viy, after thousands of years of sporadic encounters. The sum of knowledge is small, but not from lack of effort. The Devil simply has better publicity.

All reliable information regarding the Viy comes from Central Russia, from the area north of the steppes, a land of rocks. The Viy favours iron when it chooses to materialize. Iron binds but iron bends.

The Viy favours all minerals, but there are only two known instances of the Viy entwining itself with gold – once in Kyiv in 1428, where it was quickly chased away by a wise alchemist, a man who was later broken on the wheel for witchcraft, and once in Cape Town in 1863, a manifestation well-documented due to the terrible chain of disasters and murder, of raw, hand-to-hand blood vengeances (and counter-vengeances) enacted first upon and then by a family of white colonizers who kept and abused indentured Khoikhoi women. Otherwise, almost all the irrefutable materializations of the Viy, sightings supported by hard evidence, bear witness to the Viy's fancy for, and perhaps symbiosis with, iron.

There are a handful of instances recorded in Pharisaic literature and in fragments of diaries kept in Wales during the Elizabethan period, some noted in the margins of mundane ephemera – land transactions, marriage agreements – wherein contact with the Viy via copper is claimed, but none of these texts can be cross-referenced for verification.

In all the Russian literature, there is no mention of copper. Trackers of the Viy believe the so-called 'copper fallacy' to be a result of tensions in the metals markets of the two eras. Elderly Russian women call the 'copper fallacy' a European lie. One of many. How people cling to entities they fear. Devotion is neutral; like rain, it has no moral compass.

From the various source materials, current and archival, valid and questionable, a hybrid picture of the Viy emerges.

The Viy has an affinity with iron. The Viy cannot or will not cross into the material realm during the days close to or immediately following the spring equinox. The Viy has never appeared in the Western Hemisphere, although several Norwegian railroad workers brought to the American plains in the nineteenth century make joking references to 'Old Iron Eyes' in letters to their wives. It is assumed the men did so to put the fear of God into their wives and perhaps to prevent them from straying into other men's arms. This supposition is supported by the fact that the Viy is known to appear to cuckolds and cuckolders, but mostly the former.

Furthermore, testimonies describing visions of the Viy all, without deviation, relate that the Viy, no matter what other characteristics it displays, bears a pair of eyes, deep-set, with iron lids. The eyes may be dull and lifeless or hellish red, alight with fire, but the lids of the eyes are cold iron, crudely fashioned iron, and are joined together at the corners with black rivets.

The following noises are known to betray the Viy's arrival: the sound of a hammer striking an anvil, the repetitive click of coins being counted and stacked, the sound of the heel of a hobnailed boot being ground into a cobble, the contracting, pinched hiss of hot metal falling into cold water, a sword hacking at a tree trunk, a dagger being cleaned with damp salt, shotgun bursts and oil being poured into a steel bowl, entangled chains coming loose, a cannon atop a turret being ridden in jest by a drunk with spurred boots, a tin flute inexpertly played, water sloshing down a drainpipe, an empty tin can thrown from a high window, a great ship slapping against a pier, a low, long, throaty groan from a dying stag, bones broken with a crowbar, a weather vane in a hurricane, a city under siege.

The following odours are recognized as likely signs of an infestation by the Viy: the sharp smell of coffee grounds burnt on an electric stove ring, dried cloves thrown on a burning log, gasoline mixed with milk, rotting shoe leather, rotting lemon rinds, mould growing on feathers, gun oil, root of heather, rancid almonds soaked in red wine, brown puffball mushroom spores, white plaster dust, gelatin smeared on the forehead of an infant, the wicks of spent holy candles, pus, the breath of a dog that eats its own leavings, the chest-closing smell of sparks given off by steel tools grinding against stone, any underside (the bottom of a garbage can, the seat of a well-worn canvas bag), a dead river, coal ash, a dead sparrow, the Queen of Wands card aflame, a dead murderer, the sweat of a diamond cutter or the sweat of an exhausted horse, firecrackers, a new hammer, rust, always rust, fish scales drying, hard paste made from hooves (especially that used to falsify gemstones), a dead lover's blood, congealed.

From these signs will you know the Viy.

I bear witness.

Alexandar moved in. Well, that is not exactly true. Alexandar gradually occupied more and more space, in that way that men have of taking over territory, by leaving bits of their lives strewn about: a knit cap first, then a scarf, a book and another, sweatpants, a razor. By the end of November, Alexandar could be recognized in every corner. What was mine and what was his became irrelevant. I wore his scarf, I read his books. I shaved with his razor, intentionally cutting myself and not rinsing the blades, so that our blood would mingle. Sympathetic magic.

In any normal telling of the making of a couple, this would be the point where the fucking dries up, gets replaced by cuddling, movie-watching, shared meals. But we were possessed. Alexandar wanted inside me constantly, from the minute he arrived at my apartment. I rarely bothered to put on pants, unless he asked me to in advance because he had cooked up some domination game that involved me being stripped. Alexandar had a limitless imagination. There are so many small and big ways to humiliate a lover. My one black suit was dry-cleaned three times in as many weeks. My ass cheeks grew a layer of tough, flat skin, skin to match the texture of Alexandar's boots, his callused palms.

I drew the line at being tied up with the living room curtains. I had to be cautious with my money, after all. Alexandar, ever the improviser, found a roll of plastic wrap and bound me to the bedroom door frame. I shat blood for two days and still have a lower back ache. I was in love and I hated my body. What, then, was I meant to be preserving? Good health? My looks? Alexandar recognized my self-hatred and applied liberal doses of matching sentiments. He beat and fucked the hell out of me, almost. Almost. Hell always wins. Hell is everlasting, the flesh is weak. And my apartment was haunted. And Alexandar was no Saint George.

Alexandar and I grew used to the jangling noises and inexplicable odours, in the same way people become used to traffic sounds, streetcars that pass every twenty minutes, church bells, cigarette smoke. We gave as good as we got, fought back with terrible German rap music, dozens and dozens of scented candles, windows open to the freezing winds, and incense, a cathedral's worth of incense. Alexandar bought a bright tin bucket, filled it with clean white road salt, and stuck four packets of incense sticks into the salt. Light one a day, he told me. I lit five, three times a day. I had to choose between lungs full of smoke or lungs full of mist from the bogs of Hell.

The harshest sounds came from inside the wall that divided my bedroom from my living room. The wall was no thicker than a storm door, but it contained multitudes, a Hell choir. Alexandar convinced me to borrow a power drill from B, the painter, and we bored a two-euro-coin-sized hole into the wall. Alexandar peered into the hole. He saw nothing. He turned on his mobile phone and used the soft blue light of the display to look again.

'There … ' he said slowly, 'just over … ' Alexandar jumped back.

'What? What?' I asked, terrified.

Alexandar took a deep breath and looked again. He sighed. 'Oh. So it was this. Look.'

In the middle of the gloom I saw two hot red spots. Animal eyes. Hungry and flat.

Alexandar patted me on the bum. 'Look,' he said, 'look.' He began to laugh. The red dots were plastic wire covers, little fire-engine-red knobs. Harmless.

A thin stream of warm air wafted out of the hole and went straight up my nose. I sneezed. *What idiots we are*, I thought.

'And so, no spooks,' Alexandar said, shaking his head. 'Did you buy plaster?'

I sealed the hole with packing tape and covered the damage with a postcard, a reproduction of a Weegee photograph of a rear-ended car with three dead bodies inside.

'Very nice, Martin. Soon you will be much a German and I will not like you anymore.'

'The noise, the noise is the Viy,' I whispered.

'How do you say it in Canada? Don't ask the butcher to bake your bread?'

Nobody says that in Canada, I was about to say.

'We will avail ourselves with an expert.'

Avail ourselves? *Avail*? Where did he learn that word?

Alexandar stomped into the kitchen – he never walked quietly, he was forever impatient – leaving me standing beside the covered-over hole in the wall. I heard a faint wheezing sound, smelled bubbling tar. Alexandar was knocking things over, spoons and cups. He had already broken five long-stemmed wineglasses and snapped a saucepot handle in two. My big clumsy man.

'No, I since change my mind. You cannot be a German. Not ever.'

I keep having a dream about a dog. The dog is usually black, about the size of a Lab, but if the dream comes along in the early morning, the dog is yellow gold. Typical dream literalism. I'm walking the dog down a flight of steps, more like a fire escape, but wood. Steps off a deck or a balcony, at least three floors up. The dog and I get down the first set of steps easily. The dog is excited, happy to be outside, and it races ahead of me, to the end of its leash. Then it falls over, falls off the stair landing, and is hanging, choking to death, and I can't pull it back up. The dog weighs too much. I watch its feet kicking and I can see its eyes filling up with blood, popping out of its skull. There is foam coming out of the dog's mouth and running everywhere, spritzing, like a fountain. My hands are getting slippery from the dog spit and I can't pull the poor beast up. But I can't let it drop either, we're too high up. The dog just dangles, like an enormous pendulum. It won't die. I can hear it grunting and gurgling and the sound is like meat being cut with a chainsaw. I can smell the piss streaming out of the dog, then the shit. The more I pull on the leash, the harder I try to bring the dog back up to me, the heavier it gets.

When I wake up, nothing is resolved. The dog is not dead, or saved, or dropped. My hands are bent, fingers dug into my palms. My wrists throb like I've sunk them in ice. The first few times, the dream made me cry, but now I wake up angry.

Here is the problem. I am in love, and my house is being haunted, and I think the two events are related. Alexandar is tall and strong and handsome and he treats me badly in bed and like a precious gem everywhere else. He is what I've always wanted. But my mind is telling me he can't be real. I am trying so hard to love and, far tougher, to be loved, to just let it happen. But I don't trust my senses.

But I completely trust my senses, and not my education, my intellect, common sense, when it comes to the nonsensical premise that my building is haunted. Logic tells me there is no such thing as a ghost. My ears and eyes and nose know better and are more convincing. The irony is not lost on me: I am in love, just like any normal person, and I don't believe it, but I do believe I am threatened by a supernatural entity. I'm less afraid of a ghost than I am of being in love.

The first week of the new year I had a lower back ache. I think a Dutch Superman hurt my kidneys fucking me by the urinals at Mutschmann's. I didn't give a goddamn. He was worth the exorbitant price Germans pay for simple painkillers.

If any of the old gods remain, the gods of pleasure and ritual excess, they reign in Berlin. And I am nobody's 'boyfriend.' Monogamy is for teenagers and Christians.

Alexandar brought me a plastic tub of oily balm. He said he made it himself, boiling down herbs for hours and slowly stirring in boar-bone marrow and milk. "My mother's recipe for pain," he said. More like her recipe for punishment. I let him smear the gunk down my back and rub palmfuls deep into my deltoid muscles, such as they were. Naturally, Alexandar smeared his crotch with gobs of the mess and, well, I was already face down, my nose deep in a pillow. He got inside me in seconds. I thought I might shit the bed. My bowels felt like they'd been injected with a baster full of hot chilis. Alexandar held my shoulders down and asked me to lift my ass. He balled up his jeans and put the clump underneath my stomach. "Just right," he said, and banged away at my hole until his sweat covered my back, my legs, the sheets.

After he went home, I threw the sheets out and took a long, hot bath. The scum ring around the tub matched the red stains on the sheets. Rust red. Marrow red.

A day later, a letter arrived. The envelope was scratched and torn, the stamp gone. There was no postmark.

This was a letter from a madman, I decided, or a bad practical joke. I suspected Alexandar, who was capable of being the former and playing the latter. I suspected my neighbours. They must have overheard me cursing their child. Maybe the letter itself was a curse?

When all my correspondence was read and annotated by my lawyer, the man appointed to prove my insanity, a cryptologist was consulted. 'This,' she said, 'is Enochian.' The language of angels. Invented (or discovered, according to angel watchers) in the sixteenth century by John Dee, the Virgin Queen's court wizard. 'Whoever wrote this,' she said, 'really hates your client. Only psychotics and men at war talk this much about blood.'

blood blood is not enough MARTIN
spit is not enough be patient VIY is
eternal VIY is calm VIY remember VIY in the darc VIY
is noise and dust VIY is antler

felt and grit VIY is VIY VIY is VIY
other man ALEXANDAR is nothing VIY his blood is
sugar his blood is grapes his blood is a toy MARTIN is
only the door VIY is the forest MARTIN

forget VIY only in death

only in death
only in death

Today I did a massive twenty-two-card Tarot spread. The reveals were, well, revealing, to say the least. The usual contradictions popped up, of course, and the usual confirmations. But one card, off to the right of the double cruciform, really stuck with me. The Ace of Wands. Naturally. The most lonesome card in the deck. The you-must-do-it-yourself card, the card signifying solitary efforts. Or singular failures. My deck depicts the Ace of Wands as a long wand with a clear diamond on top, a solid black opaque diamond on the bottom. The clear one has ten tiny squares hanging over it, arranged in a pyramid – one square, then two, then three, then four – and the squares are also transparent, empty. I take these to be aspirational ... what? ... signifiers? The clear-at-the-top/dark-at-the-bottom dynamic is pretty obvious. Don't sink. Don't go too low or the darkness will overcome you, spear you even. The black diamond is a warning. Nothingness is not benign. Nothingness has sharp edges. The thing I find mystifying about the card is the hand that holds the wand. In the illustration, the hand, obviously male, is emerging from a thin cloud. It makes a fist around the wand, in the dead centre. But the fist it makes is formed so that the thumb covers the index finger. It's as if the hand is refusing to give a direction to the reader, is neutral in the clear/black battle. But then why is there a hand at all? Why is the wand not simply presented on top of a plain background? Who is the guiding force? God? The reader? I feel like this card is deceptive, to me, the reader, and also to itself. There is no such thing as a neutral gesture.

Which brings me to Alexandar. I am starting to wonder if he is intentionally trying to drive me mad. And I don't mean that in the sexy-fun way, the madly-in-love way. I mean it literally. Insane. Why he would want to do that, I have no idea.

But, then, how much do I really know about Alexandar? Next to nothing. We fuck and we talk, but the talk is always about anything but Alexandar. Politics to poltergeists. But never the ghost man in my bed. He is forever telling stories. Blowing smoke up my ass (that part is literal – have you ever had a 'smoky'? it feels amazing).

Stories and parables. Tales with triple meanings, seven meanings, limitless meanings. He is like an archive of old pre-Christian European monster tales. These stories are never linear, but they all have firm conclusions. Lots of lopped-off heads and the like. Giant lake snakes and snow queens, eternal fires, rocks that whisper the names of the dead, swords made of oak leaves. There is a kind of warped, internal logic to the stories, and a stern morality. And he fucks like he talks, as if he's enacting an atavistic ritual, sex magyck. It's fun, it's exhausting.

Honestly, how hard would it be to drive me out of my mind? It's in the family, as they say. For my father, reality was, at best, a nuisance. He had other priorities. He lied for fun. And then it wasn't fun anymore, it was just an easier way to live, to be in the world, to be in the world without worrying about the consequences of your actions.

When I was about ten, I developed a terror of ghosts, good old-fashioned sheet-head ghosts. I don't know what triggered the phobia, probably a television show – television was full of shows about the supernatural in the seventies. And I was such a trusting child. From the day I told my father that I thought our house was haunted, I heard tapping sounds in the night. It was him, of course, rapping his fat knuckles on the walls.

I sort of knew it was him and I sort of didn't know at the same time. I would literally scream, cry, beg him to stop. He would laugh. Mum would scold him. And half an hour later the tapping would start again. He swore it was not him.

One time he brought a Bible into my bedroom and put his hand on top and swore he was not tapping on the walls. After which, there was more tapping. This went on for months, a whole winter. He woke me up at all hours. I fell asleep in school once and got sent home because I couldn't keep my head up. Mum had a terrible fight with him, but he kept on knocking. Eventually he got bored and moved on to other things. If I remember properly, it was sugar. He banned all sugar from the house; I forget now what prompted that particular lunacy.

So here I am again, living with a man who taps on walls. Am I that obvious, such an easy target? Do men just look at me and think: *This guy, this guy I can play tricks on until he snaps, this guy will amuse me for a while, before another little bird comes along, another fragile thing to torment and perhaps love a little too, until a prettier, stupider bundle of nerves slinks along?*

People treat you in precisely the manner you teach them to treat you. Alexandar is just my latest mirror. Ignoring my own godfuckingawful romantic history isn't viable, even if I've run away from home. Wherever you are, there you are. How I hate simple truths. They trip me up every time.

I'm broken, and, like all mammals with a sense of self vs. other, I expect the world to reflect me. So, I break my world. Berlin is not a cure. Berlin is not enough.

If there's a Hell below, we all gonna go, as Curtis Mayfield sang. Poor bastard.

Alexandar was asleep beside me. He took up most of the bed. I didn't mind. I watched him sleep. Three long breaths, one short breath. The short breath caught, a hiccup. Huff, huff, huff, exhale, catch, quick exhale, puff, repeat. I was enchanted, ridiculous.

I watched Alexandar sleep. His shoulder muscles were beautiful, curls of marble. The back of his neck was freshly shaved. I rested my thumb on the pulse point under his jaw, the burble of blood. I counted to ten, to twenty-five. I kissed the top of his head. I found a small nest of pale hair between his shoulder blades and licked the skin around the hair with the wet tip of my tongue. A moat around a forest. His nerves reacted, but he didn't wake. I didn't want to wake him. I wanted to know him as he had known me so many, many times, awake and asleep, as a helpless, witless body, a mass and weight without consciousness, as a toy.

'Tonight you're mine … completely,' I sung softly. Maybe this was love, finally, love: not ownership but an earned dominion, trading trusts. And so very fragile. Any sound, the smallest pinch, would break the spell. People talk about love as a high, a high so distracting one drops plates and laughs, knocks over bookshelves and laughs, bursts into tears at the sight of puppies playing. They're wrong. Love is focus, love is magnification. Love is noticing: noticing his dropped hairs, his careless lumbering gait, the white half-moons at the base of the beloved's fingernails, the beloved's end-of-the-day scent. Noticing too much. When you are in love, any detail, all detail, is equal to any other detail. Love is a lack of discernment plus physical attraction plus time plus habit times two bodies in reasonable proximity. Love is the opposite of choice, of self-determination. There was a man in my bed who was certain enough of my care for him to fall asleep, to let go of his day, to kick at tangled sheets and snort and draw closer for warmth, to huff, huff, huff, then exhale, to be at my mercy. If love is so easy, so feral, why did it come to me so late?

Alexandar slept and I watched. He would fall asleep so fast. I envied his slack biceps, his dropped stomach, how he aged ten years when he slept, became old and soft and short of breath. Alexandar asleep and Alexandar awake were not the same man. To think, he used to frighten me with his rough needs.

I could have taken him, there, then, held him against me and been inside him in seconds. He might have woken, we might have reversed positions. Alexandar awake could flip me over his shoulder. Alexandar awake could hold me down with one arm. Alexandar awake was master, benevolent or cruel, as he pleased. I would need to be swift, be in the right position, legs aligned to his legs, my pelvis below his tailbone, my cock full and head empty, with both my hands on his shoulders and my lungs flush with new air. I pulled back the sheets, slid my body down, low to his centre. I was covered in sweat. Alexandar's ass was dry, leathery where the buttocks meet the legs. I dribbled spit on my cock. Alexandar's ass was covered in short, stiff hairs, bristles, little ticklers that reached for the tip of my cock, teasing. I wondered if he shaved his bum. And then he woke up. It was my fault. I let a question, a stupid question, enter my mind, and Alexandar could read minds.

'Hey, you, little teufel. What is here? The piggy's tail is straight.'

Alexandar reached behind his back, took my cock in his hand, pumped it until I came, came all over my stomach, onto the sheets. I felt a drop land in my left armpit. I shivered, embarrassed, as if I'd wet the bed.

'No big ideas in the middle of the night, good?'

Alexandar gave my cock a hard squeeze, then another. He pulled me closer to him. He tucked my cock between his legs and tensed. I was caught. He rested a hand on the small of my back. His hand was heavy, hot as an iron. In seconds, he was asleep again. I was sticky and stupid and my scalp was itchy. I hugged Alexandar as if the bed were shrinking.

A light flicked on somewhere in the building and the bedroom window turned pale blue. Blue and flecked. Flecks of silver, copper, gold, abalone. Plus dust diamonds, icicle white. A treasure mound, a thieves' cave, trapped in glass.

Alexandar left early, before seven. I got up, turned on the bathroom light, rinsed out my mouth. The dried cum on my stomach was as thick and solid as cooled hot glue. I peeled it off in strips. The skin was bare underneath, hairless, like a waxed leg.

Later, I found a note on the kitchen table. Alexandar's handwriting was blocky but sure, all capitals and robotically precise.

You are out of coffee. You are run out of hair soap. It is snowing, and so I need to use two of your strong Canadian socks. Thank you. Thank you for a nice night. You are also cute. Your sink water smells like smoke. Call me when it is dark. You give me a terrible idea. Fun for us both.

A.

My tea is milky and tastes like raw almonds.

My apartment was flooded – luckily nothing was damaged, but the inconvenience and the cleanup. I hired a cleaning woman, which I've never done in my life. I have always felt guilty about paying people for services, people like a house-cleaner. It seems stupid now, that misplaced class guilt. Everybody has to work, after all.

Well, everybody except half the artists I know from home, who were all fucking there that winter – C, of course, always C, and S, perennially, and B, again, and then, during the film festivals, all the Lesbian Heiresses of Toronto. I've said it before and here I say it again: take any ten 'successful' artists from Toronto, and six of them come from family money. How else is it done? Funny how they all get government cash to top up the pile left by Mommy and Daddy. Grants, and tenure. Tenured Heiresses. Now, there's a band name.

But anyway, I left Toronto because it was making me bitter … Still not cured! I just don't know where one goes anymore to get away from people. A. was all over me to see his big performance at HAU. I know what he wanted: press. And he was right. I could have sold an article on his dance-video whats-its to any number of magazines or newspapers. I just didn't want to.

How do I tell these people that, yes, on many levels my disdain is personal (I cannot recall ever, ever seeing B at anything I have ever done, big or small), but ultimately my disdain is keenest for the entire art-coverage industry (can anything so small and underwhelming be called an 'industry'?), that I'm fed up with looking at pins and sticks and writing thousands of words, lies, describing pillars and redwoods?

In a way, whatever an artist is making no longer matters. It's the translation, not the text, that matters. How do I tell people, even people I like and whose work I admire, that my bowels are empty, that I am all out of shit? Enough, enough.

The cleaning woman vacuumed the walls. Yes, the walls. She had a dozen different types of cleaning sprays. One for mould, one for dust, one for ground-in dirt, one for glass, one for furniture. If I understood her cavewoman English, she cleans churches, churches are her specialty. I've seen the churches here – most of them are now community centres or youth drop-in spots or government offices. Polishing the pews is likely low on the priority list, if the pews are still there.

Anyway, then my apartment smelled like a hotel. Alexandar came over for late-afternoon cake (read 'cake' any way you like) and I forbade him to smoke inside anymore. He made such faces. Like taking three steps outside to the courtyard, which was already in bloom, was the fucking Bataan Death March. What a wife I'd become.

(I went to a puppy-play party. I had never seen anything less sexy and more stupid in my life. About thirty guys, half pretending to be dogs and half pretending to believe that their 'dogs' were dogs. Of course, it was all about being a 'bad dog' and getting punished for misbehaviour, for not obeying commands, but the foreplay before the bad-dog punishment was elaborate, deeply boring, and went on for hours. Imagine a bunch of naked men crawling around on all fours, with rubber butt plugs shaped like dog tails stuck up their asses, pretending to chase a ball, or pretending to play-fight over a rope chew toy, and barking, of course, and eating out of dog bowls, of course, and rolling over to have their stomachs rubbed.)

I know all S/M is bad theatre, but this was bad improv, open-stage night at the Second City. This one guy was clearly a Down's syndrome person. Yes, for real. I was not sure if he was playing or had been convinced he was a dog, a real dog. Kind of alarming.

Alexandar was thrilled by the whole spectacle. I asked him why he liked it so much and he said it was because if I had grown up in a culture, like his, that celebrated clowns as artists, I would find puppy play both sexy and funny. I swore that if he ever asked me to eat out of a bowl or threatened me with a rolled-up newspaper the relationship would be over. I had my limits. And I could make bad theatre all by myself, thanks.

The bottom line is that no matter where you go, there you are (I forget who said that, but it sounds like Yogi Berra). I am rut-prone.

Sure, I saw new things every day, but I also did the same things every day. Not even a flood could dislodge me from my ways. Or a strange and beautiful man. I defeated geography, language, culture, climate. I was my habits, my grudges, my enthusiasms, my own best friend and my own wrong crowd.

Two postcards arrived, one oversized, one standard.

The standard card bore a photo of a small, brown-skinned boy dressed as a servant, a miniature Moor, complete with an enormous, onion-shaped turban, billowy harem pants, and shoes with curled toes. A bracelet of bells dangled from his wrist. The larger card was plain, minimal. A blue dot on a scuffed white background, a blue dot so dark it was almost black. What is blue called when it is deeper than navy blue? Submarine blue. Under-the-ice blue. Drowned blue.

A six-line poem was handwritten on the message side of the Moor-boy card. The poem was broken into three neatly spaced couplets but was otherwise incomprehensible. I guessed it was a poem from the formal line breaks and spacing, the nursery-rhyme format. The text was Enochian.

At my trial, a translation was provided. German justice is nothing if not thorough.

Brother Liar, friend of all
Son and Brother, to me both

I sing your Name, your Name is Axe
I hear your Heart! Beg Mercy

Your Name is Knife, Your Name is Sword
Brother Liar, feed

The blue dot card's verso was covered in messy X's and + signs, each one made with a different pen. All the figures had been drawn and then roughly redrawn, carved into, at least four or five times, a few perhaps as many as a dozen times. Ink over ink over ink. Black stars.

The figures ran together in a mad chain, the bottom right chop of each X touching the left prong of each +. In the dead centre of the card sat an exquisite photorealist drawing of a small blue flower, an image so delicate, so faint, it looked like it had been crafted with a nail clipping or an eyelash.

As if winter in Berlin isn't creepy enough, I thought. *It would kill my secret correspondent to send me a jolly gnome or a late Valentine, a noble stag tramping through the snow?*

I considered burning the cards, burning the whole lot of mystery missives, the ever-growing bundle, the psychotic paper trail filling up my apartment. I'd host a bonfire, with fireworks and meaty snacks and plenty of clean, clear vodka to purge the sinuses, cauterize my liver.

But who would come? My fellow expats had all gone home, back to Spruce Lake and Saint-Hyacinthe, back to Bathurst and Oakville, to their parents' well-heated homes, to cable television and Player's Lights, to the 'Huron Carol' and sledding with nephews and nieces, back to nice, back to sweet, back to tidy, back to CBC Radio and fatty rum eggnog, Christmas specials on the television and Boxing Day pleasure drives, back to healthy, back to teacup manners and Midnight Mass, back to where the money, the real money, always waits, at the dinner table.

Unfortunately, my family had nothing to give me. My family wouldn't know how to make me comfortable. My family would never try. Besides, I had Alexandar to think of, Alexandar plus

Bear-mas at Woof Bar, the Leather Santa toy drive at Mutsch-mann's, Aktion Club Piss-mas, lonely men on the internet who would be grateful for a Christmas fuck from anybody, and the charming German tradition of yuletide birchings. I would put my shoes beside my bed and wait for candies and oranges, marzipan treats shaped like pigs and chimney sweeps, bottles of red wine peppered with cloves and apple rinds. I would hang a paper star in my window and light the Advent candles. Christmas would come to me.

Standing by the mailbox, I pressed both cards against my forehead, like a cheap magician about to reveal the lost, up-his-sleeve ace of spades, to tell the name of the audience member who just had a baby, to grow twisted horns. Nothing. I felt nothing. But a virus is a silent creature. Neurochemicals travel on felted feet. We're lucky, us busy types, to stop and sit long enough to hear our own heartbeats. Anything smaller, the quieter transactions – food turned to sugar turned to cells turned to blood, blood turned against itself – escape us. Which is why even children know not to touch filthy things, fondle dead flies, or make pies with their own shit.

I went back inside and began writing a note to my father, who'd seen his last winter four years before and appreciated nothing that was done to cheer him through the season. He was a spectacularly ungrateful human being, right until the end. I was halfway into a description of the actors who play Soviet soldiers at Checkpoint Charlie and charge five euros for a photograph before I remembered that my father had died as he lived, in bed.

I need a nap, I thought. *I need a drink*. My head felt like it was stuck on the end of a pike. I needed a drink, in bed. My father was dead and I had yet to cry. I was coming down with a fever. What killed my father? I don't even know. I never asked. Go ahead, skull, explode. Be done with it. I'm writing letters to the dead. A pill, a drink, a bit of time under the blankets, and I'd be right as rain. Was it a stroke? I didn't go to his funeral. The dead seemed to be writing to me, so why not? What did Dad always say? Whatever doesn't kill you will try, try again. Clonazepam, aquavit, duvet. I could feel my scalp stretching, stretching to hold my brain together. All the bones in my neck were brittle, ice on glass. I wanted. I wanted a good stiff. I wanted a good. Mother of God, he'd been dead for four years. Don't dream. Don't dream. Let the fever burn you down.

I don't remember the rest of the day. I don't remember putting the postcards in my front window, message side out. I don't remember cleaning the bread knife. I don't remember wrapping the bread knife in a green wool scarf. I don't remember hiding the bread knife under the bed.

I think about all the letters I sent from Berlin and I'm disgusted by how much I took for granted.

And I don't mean any of the things people who are incarcerated always say they long for, the things they never took time to notice: a gentle breeze caressing the face, the warm tingle of sunshine on the shoulders, sex, cooking your own food, long walks on beaches, the scent of pine. No, I mean the luxury to complain. The charm of having mild problems. The ability to make your life appear more interesting by virtue of uncertainty, disquiet.

My days are nothing but certain now. I live in stasis. I am the quietest, best-behaved madman in all of Germany, perhaps Europe. The prison is a kindly place, full of helpful and patient caregivers. I am fed meals heavy on carbohydrates, to make me slower, sleepier. I am fed pills, which I quite enjoy. For a treat, I will pretend to take my pills for several days and then swallow the lot all at once. The hallucinations are vivid and exact and often highly metaphorical, as easy to decipher as the dream of flying, and rippingly pornographic. And I can safely say that I am truly fond of several of my minders. What is a friend, after all, but someone you talk to every day?

I've always been good at connecting. The trick is to ask questions, make the object of your affection feel he is unique. Leap on his every word. The things I am able to get out of the people hired to pull my mind apart surprise even me. The qualifications for being the key holder who keeps killers and rapists, firebugs and flashers, the likes of me, continually occupied and forever out of the way are, apparently, not so extensive.

In the outside world, I could have any one of my jailers over for tea, and a couple of them I could just have, so to speak. The men are the easiest. They have to try so much harder to prove that they are caring and sensitive.

Also, there is the obvious truth that hovers over all of my conversations with my male watchers, in particular the better-educated ones: any man alive considers committing murder at least half a dozen times a day. Men like violence. Men's minds are wired for fantasizing. Two plus two.

I killed Alexandar. Slowly, brutally, carelessly. His death was messy, long, dragged out, and idiotic. He didn't need to die. There are a hundred easier ways to kill the romance. But I would have my luxuries.

They don't warn you about late winter, the Berliners. Smart, really. Nobody in his right mind would stay here in January if he knew what he was in for. Like me.

February doesn't arrive, it lands, on top of you, like a wet cold towel or a thick hide, and stays. The sunlight lasts about three hours a day, on a good day. The rest of the day is neither sunset nor sunrise. The rest of the day is grey stasis. Dreamy, but without the colours of dreams. Restful, but without the refreshment of sleep.

The shops are empty, the bars are empty, the sex clubs are empty, and the subway is full, morning and midnight, full of people staring at their shoes, playing with their phones, looking anywhere but out the train window, because the sky is just too flat, too monotone, a cement ceiling. Where are they all going?

Perhaps there is another Berlin, the winter Berlin, and I just haven't found it yet, a city within the city where people are jolly and engaged and drunk and sexy. A walled garden. A national secret, warm and bright and beery. With limited occupancy. Locals only. Strict door policy. No photographs.

New Year's Eve was full of promise. The city goes mad. Violently mad. Toddlers carry Roman candles the size of baseball bats up and down the streets, looking for matches, an adult with a lighter. Grannies and twinks get loaded and hang off each other, singing and stumbling. The corner shops sell very convincing plastic guns that shoot firecrackers. Kids loiter in the subway and wait for the train doors to open so they can throw chains of lit gunpowder caps into the cars, at the passengers. The security guards watch and laugh. Dresses catch fire, and everybody laughs. Paper party hats catch fire, and everybody laughs.

Alexandar gave me a potted plant for New Year, a cluster of four-leaf clovers in a plastic silver champagne bucket, a good-luck token. And he brought me a bottle of caraway schnapps, and a pig made out of marzipan, and a stick figure made out of black pipe cleaners – it's meant to represent a chimney sweep, a sign of a fresh start, a clean hearth. The chimney sweep carries a gold foil ladder and a plastic red mushroom. Luck tokens carrying luck tokens. He was so adorable when he presented all this childish tat to me (he is not prone to silliness, ever), so boyish. He really wanted me to have 'a proper German New Year,' which I took to mean more – that he wanted me to be in his world, nonsense and all, trash and traditions. I'm in love, it's awful, it's great, it's easy, it's a mountain. I don't know what to do. I can't live here forever, and I get a very strong sense that Alexandar could never leave Germany, maybe even for legal reasons. I still don't know exactly what he does for a living, but I think it might involve loading and unloading trucks in the middle of the night. Or watching over the men who do. He really could be a mule. There is an air of menace about him, and he dresses like a New York Italian, all dark flash and fitted jackets, shoes spit-shined (usually my spit), a diamond here, a diamond there. Mafia chic lite, without the grease.

Aunty J predicted I would fall in love in Berlin and never come back. I said to him, all drunk bluster, 'That'll be the fucking day!' Well, now it is the fucking day. That startling, glorious, hallelujah-choir, UFO-landing, five-cannon-salute the-king-is-dead-long-live-the-king fucking day. Goddammit. What am I to do?

People who predict the future should be shot. Too late now. I feel like a newly adopted cat: Where do my loyalties lie? Who keeps me warm, who feeds me? Which leg do I rub against? Where are the exits?

I can hear my Canadian self all the way across the Atlantic: *Martin, let's put this on the table and process it, cut the situation up into manageable pieces and make it whole again.* But I don't want to do that. I've lived my whole life so carefully, so full of plans and Plan Bs. I have a few more months to be reckless before my money runs out, and I want to be reckless, desperately reckless and even self-destructive, an idiot, a man with no plan. It's my last chance. I'll be fifty before the decade ends. Forget Time not being on my side, Time is standing in front of me with a switchblade and a mean look.

I promise to think about the situation in the spring, maybe.

Alexandar is blowing on the back of my ear. Puff, long sigh, puff. I pretend not to notice. He's adorable, he's annoying. He's rough, he's sweet. He's a brat, he looks out for me. I'm in bed with a teenage boy, I'm in bed with a battle-scared veteran. I'm in love with a man, I'm in love with a puppy, love is a magic show, love is surgery, a microscopic camera in a tube burrowing through my stomach. I'm in over my head, I have never been more comfortable.

'Where are you, Martin? Mr. Martin? Hello, naked man? Make me laugh.'

Question, question, question, demand. The Alexandar rag. I'm learning to hear the real question, the real request. I turn over.

'I'm thinking about all the years I wasted trying to be dignified.'

'What is dignified?'

'Your English gets worse the closer it gets to dawn.'

'Hmm. And so?'

'*Dignified* is a word people use to say they are scared when they don't want to admit that they are scared.'

'So, a word for lies?'

'Yes and no. Imagine that you are very angry with somebody, but you don't want anybody to know that you are angry, because being angry doesn't look good, being angry is not attractive, so you say instead that you are going to be dignified, you are going to hide your real feelings to keep yourself from looking stupid or out of control.'

'Hmmm. Hide-and-seek.'

'Hide-and-seek. I used to be so angry all the time, and nobody ever knew.'

'Maybes you are still having anger?' Alexandar pulls me close. His nipples are covered in short, sharp bristles. I wonder why he shaves his nipples. Europeans are crazy.

'No, not me. No. I'm a lamb.'

Alexandar buries his nose in my neck. I twist my head and look up. And I see a fox, in the corner where the wall meets the ceiling, a fox with all four paws stretched out, back paws on the walls beneath it, front paws on the ceiling, muzzle pointed down, eyes bright as new leather. No, not a fox. Foxes don't smile. Foxes don't have faces that are half red and half black. Foxes don't whistle. Foxes don't levitate.

I am not afraid. The fox-monster arches its back. Two clumps of fur form cones on either side of its spine. The cones turn into horns, then into wings. Beautiful brick-orange wings. The wings spread, dust falls from the under-fur. Pure black dust. Soot. The red half of the monster's face turns black, the black half red. How it smiles. How it looks at me, mother to child. I am not afraid.

Alexandar shivers. He is awake and not awake, falling into sleep. I cover his shoulders with my arms, press him closer. He is shaking now. I wrap him in our blanket, uncovering half my body. It's what lovers do, make small sacrifices. I am not cold, quite the opposite. I feel hot, drunk-headed hot. The monster winks. The fur on its belly moves, first flattening then rising, a spike of hair here, a wave beside it. The fur makes a picture, a relief, images form in the negative spaces, the shadows between the stiffened tufts. An eye, a nose, a doubled chin, another eye. My face.

I kiss Alexandar on the forehead. He is unconscious. He breathes like a running dog, tongue out, lungs never full enough.

The fox-angel drops its tongue, down, past the doorknob, lower, to the floor, across the room, over the sheets, behind my head. The tongue is meaty, sweating, smooth on the top and pocked on the bottom, a muscle flayed, a rope-ladder rung. The tip of the tongue rises above Alexandar's head, then darts down, arrow sharp at the end. The point of the tongue licks Alexandar's hairline, right to left, sopping his brow. Alexandar stops breathing, seconds pass. He coughs, a harsh bark. His breath smells like boiled meat, pepper, and gasoline. He rolls over, reaches behind his back for my forearm. I squeeze him, squeeze him, press and press. He is so cold.

I kiss the back of Alexandar's neck, run my lips across his shoulders. He is so cold. The fox-monster's tongue snaps back into its head. A key sliding into a lock. As suddenly as it arrived, the beast disappears, paw and muzzle and fur wings and fur mirror, tongue and tail, all at once. Alexandar is dead to the world, snoring.

In the morning, Alexandar shaves. I watch from the bed, lazy and comfortable. I watch him shave while I play with my cock. I have no dignity.

'Ach! What is that?'

'Did you cut yourself?'

'What do you do when I am asleep? Bang my head slap-slap on the wall?'

Alexandar examines his face in the bathroom mirror. His chin is shaved on one side, slathered with foam on the other. He is too amazed to notice. He turns on the light above the sink. In the middle of his forehead a lump is swelling, big as a two-euro coin, big as the business end of a pistol.

'If you are making to kill me, don't take so long, yes okay?'

'Planning.'

'Ouch!' Alexandar pokes the bump. The bubble of flesh is red at the centre.

'Planning to kill you. That's how you say it. Planning. Come back to bed.'

'Ach no! If you are doing to kill me I want to die like your American cowboys, with my boots on, thank you. Only women and babies die in bed.'

I get up and examine Alexandar's forehead. A tiny vein runs across the middle of the bump. The blood in the vein is yellow, stale, and spent. Alexandar fusses and I let him go.

'You'll live.'

I get back into bed and watch Alexandar finish shaving. A clump of red fur floats past my face. I catch it and rub the hairs between my palms.

My fingers are curling in on themselves, turning my hands into claws, or paws. I am always making a fist. When I wake up in the morning, my left index finger is bent in half, fixed downward. I unhinge the middle knuckle with a quick pull. The pain comes later. An hour later, half a day later. The pain comes with the headaches.

My temples are growing concave, as if being sucked hollow from the inside. Where does the flesh go? All over my stomach and up the outer sides of my thighs, little craters form. You can fit a penny inside the deeper pits. I sit in a hot bath each night before bed and count the holes. Thirty-one, then seventeen, then forty-nine, then only five. New bellybuttons, every day. But who are my new mothers?

I need to leave this apartment, need sun and air and green leaves, to see romping dogs and worry about dirt under my nails, smell fried food, hear café chatter. I need to be among the lively, joyful, and foolish – the living.

At first I was entertained by all the inanimate objects in my borrowed apartment, their needling antics, their seeming mindfulness. I thought they displayed a kind of liveliness, a kind of life energy. But there is no joy in a doorknob that turns itself all day long, or a curtain that flutters and snaps beside a closed window, or a plate that stands on its rim and spins like a coin, no razzle-dazzle in light bulbs that blink three long, two short, three long, for hours.

I feel, now, the hate underneath the teasing, understand the difference between play and attack, tickle vs. jab. This borrowed apartment wants me gone – it knows its own mind, and it knows it wants Alexandar here and not me. The beams and floorboards have weighed their options and made a choice: Alexandar is tall and handsome and his blood is as rich as royal jelly; I am neither and I sleep in the afternoons. A haunted house has one virtue: it knows its own mind. But I want Alexandar too. Let the doorknobs jangle, the toilet belch. I've broken bigger furniture, bent thicker iron bars. Slow war is my specialty.

I need to leave this apartment. Bergmanstrasse is close, 143 steps away. Bergmanstrasse is full of cute shops, cute cafés, cute couples with dogs, with snoring babies. I'll buy a book, a book in English. Something thrilling, from Scandinavia, a novel with a soulful cop protagonist, a cop who listens to opera and misses his dead wife. Basic distraction never fails me.

The couples are here, the dogs in sweaters are here, the Bergmanstrasse specialty shops filled with gewgaws from India are here. And so are the jumbies. The sprites. The fiends. A field mouse with a flaming head, sitting on top of a stoplight, giggling. Two jackdaws reading the newspaper and licking their green lips. A red tulip with white eyes sprouts from a car mirror. My new friend the fox-demon walks beside me, his mouth spilling over with orange coals. In front of Cuccuma Café, a choir of rabbits, thirty or forty, then one hundred, the number inflates and contracts, hold sprigs of pink heather and sing David Bowie's 'Heroes' backwards. Several of the rabbits have fangs, naturally. I sip my coffee and wait. Beside me sits a bald, purplish man, a cheerful sort. He is gradually shrinking, becoming baby-sized. Sparks blink in his eyes. Not all demons are evil. The demon ranks have their idiots too.

At the Turkish grocery store, between the cans of tomato paste, a child, a pale ugly child, thin as a sheet of paper, darts and bends, a vertical snake. I'm surrounded. I need never be lonely again.

'**F**or you this is not much money, so.'

'I don't have the kind of money you think I have.'

'You Amer–. You North Americans. Five hundred euros and burn your teeth with lasers but fifty euros not to save your soul.'

'Here we go again.'

'No, not again, true. When you always have money you don't understand money.'

'I don't always have money. I've never always had money. I don't want to argue about money.'

'No, we cannot have disagreements about money because money has not the meaning for you. So for you why argue?'

'Anyway.'

'Anyway. Whatever. Who is caring. Forget it totally. Going forward. Blah and blah.'

I had to laugh. Where did Alexandar learn 'going forward'? Just as suddenly as it started, as all our arguments started, the disagreement was over. Alexandar punched me in the shoulder. What a boy.

'Do you know her? Will it work?'

'She went to first school with my mother. A hundred years ago. Or looks like so. It will work.'

'Okay. Fifty euros. You can buy my drinks for a week after.'

'I am the lucky most husband in all of Berlin!'

'If I'm paying, I get to be the husband.'

'Not tonight. Turn over.'

A week later Nadja arrived, as agreed, exactly at seven thirty in the morning, and went to work. Nadja the exorcist.

Nadja was tall for a woman, a woman born in or near the First World War. She smiled as she walked around the apartment, the first, fourth, and eleventh time. For a whole hour, she paced, sticking her nose into the corners, under the radiators, behind the toilet.

She smiled and sometimes chuckled while she overturned every plate in the plate rack. She whistled into the coffee cups. She politely asked me to take all the plants out of the apartment and leave them in the frozen courtyard. Leave them to die. She asked for a plastic bag and then collected all the candles, new and half-burnt, and asked me to wrap the bag in a clean blanket.

In her last sweep, she licked her right index finger and made the sign of the cross on every chair seat and pillow. Her spit was yellow-brown. I looked away.

Nadja sat in the dead centre of the living room floor and unbuttoned her blouse. Her breasts were enormous, more long than plump, and sleek, unmarked by time. All the skin below her creping neck was the same, taut and fresh-looking, youthful, unmarked by clogged veins, brown moles, or creases. Clean living? Or a deal with the devil?

With her stage, the bare floor freshly wiped with lemon juice, carefully set, and her props – a silver bowl with fresh, salted water, a clean rag on which she asked me to rub my bare, stinky feet, three red tulips not yet open, and a new can of tobacco – arranged in a semicircle beside her creaking knees, Nadja began. I was told to stand in the kitchen, as far away from her as I could get without leaving her sight, and to think of my mother, or a church, or a field of wildflowers, or a bright white light, 'holy things, holy places, clean and good.'

Do not, I was warned, under any circumstances, think about words or numbers, letters of the alphabet or sums of money. And do not, ever, until she was back outside and on her own way home, look at a clock.

Do not, Nadja warned, dig the demon a fresh tunnel. Vermin are crafty enough.

Nadja made two fists and set her knuckles on the floor, arms straight down. She slowly moved her body back and forth, her bottom flattening on her heels when she tilted backward. With every forward motion, she barked out a single word, in a language I did not understand, a language that sounded like Latin but had no melody, no fluidity. A language that also sounded like Mandarin but had no vowel sounds. A guttural language not from the gut, a language that poured out of her limbs, her muscles, a wet, spittle-fed language that every three words turned brittle, dry, that suddenly sparked and sizzled. A language both alien and maternal.

Forty words, forty back-and-forth shuffles. Then silence. Nadja closed her eyes and lifted the bowl. She poured the salted water between her breasts. She did not flinch or shiver. She wiped herself with the rag, then tied it into three knots. She tossed the rag backwards over her head. 'Matches! Now! Matches!'

I reached for a box of matches and began to walk toward her. 'Stop! Throw!'

I threw the box at her head. She caught it in one simple, exact gesture, with one hand. Her eyes were shut tight, as if she were being blinded by a bright light.

Nadja emptied the can of tobacco on the floor in front of her, making a little brown mountain. She lit one match and dropped it onto the mound, then another, then another, until the pile was smouldering. She blew on the embers. The house filled with coarse, furious smoke, the smell of a barn on fire. Nadja began her recitation again, clapping between each word. Her palms, rough as rope, turned bright red.

I sat on the kitchen floor, trying to get a clean breath. The smoke hovered over my head, sending out little tendrils, searching wisps. The smoke was looking for me.

On the thirty-ninth word, Nadja grabbed the tulips and roughly shoved them down the back of her skirt, wiping her ass with the stems and petals until all three flowers were shredded. Again, she tossed the mangled handful behind her, backwards over her head. Her body shook.

A horrid blast of words poured out of Nadja's mouth, an incomprehensible stream of abuse directed at the walls, the floor, me, the ceiling, the air itself. I heard two words in French, or thought I did, and one word in English, my name. I was certain I also heard German, Russian, and Italian, in fragments. But I was not supposed to think about words.

A pipe behind the kitchen sink broke through the plaster. A pipe running between the water heater and the bedroom radiator ballooned, then turned red-hot. A deafening bang, the sound of an iron hammer hitting an anvil, shook the floorboards. Nails loosened from the walls, furniture disassembled itself, every light bulb in the apartment glowed green, blue, green, red, blue, green. The next day, I found eleven dead birds in the courtyard.

Nadja pissed on the floor. Her urine was dull and clouded, a dirty yellow. Clots formed in the pools. I gagged at the smell, the stench of infection, of old dirty wax, of sweat and pencil lead, of stale meat on wet bone. Nadja stood up, quick as a rabbit. Her skirt was sopping wet, clinging to her legs. She held her hands over her head and smacked her palms together over and over. The smoke cleared. The floorboards shuddered and barked, belched dust out of the cracks, but Nadja remained upright, clapping harder. Her palms began to blister. A little greenish cloud of smoke lingered over her head, teasing strands of her hair until whole clumps stood upright. She never flinched. The cloud broke into three, then six, smaller clouds. The six puffs became twelve, twenty-four, forty-eight, and then nothing but trails of smoke, skinny green ghosts.

Nadja lowered her hands, stepped gingerly over the burnt tobacco pyre, and walked into the kitchen carrying her blouse. She handed me the blouse. 'Do this. Fingers hurt.'

I did up her blouse, looking away from her shining breasts.

'Water, with thank you.'

Nadja drank four full glasses of water, then patted me on the back.

'And so good. Maybe work. Pray God. No meat, six days. No wine, six days. No fucks, six days. No music, six days. Don't go in car. Don't hit children. Six days. Maybe work.'

'Maybe?'

'Hmm. And so. Fifty euros. Now.'

Nadja pulled a smart phone out of her skirt pocket. She put one arm around my shoulder, pulled me to her, and lifted the phone up to our faces. The phone flashed.

Nadja looked at the image on the screen. She smiled. 'For web page.' She smacked the back of my head. 'You good boy. Boy with old face. Old-man face. And so.'

I paid the exorcist with a new fifty-euro note. She kissed me on both cheeks and left. Alexandar phoned me an hour later. I could hear a video game plinking in the background, the sound of men laughing, a Turkish pop song.

'All is good?'

'Maybe so.'

The Tarot whispers. The Tarot does not shout. The Tarot is impatient, the Tarot is stupidly eternal, like stone. The Tarot hates the hand that deals it. The Tarot is subject, the Tarot is indifferent. The Tarot is law, the Tarot cannot be trusted. The Tarot is just a deck of cards, the Tarot is a weather vane. The Tarot whispers. I put my fingers in my ears.

The Sun, then the Tower. A Ten of Cups.

The Sun's face is resigned, a set face. Eyes partially hooded, full lips slightly downcast, nose flat, eyebrows casually arched. The Sun's face is surrounded by rays: eight hard points, the tips of daggers, eight curled points, peeling leaves or the death end of a scimitar. Underneath the Sun grow two fairy rings, circles of sparse grass. A naked boy and a naked girl, perfectly formed as cherubs, but obviously sexed, hold naked hands. The boy looks at you, at the reader. The girl looks at the boy. She has made her choice. This scene is not sexual but the opposite, neutered, as erotic as a washed plate. Behind the children a low brick wall supports five bursting sunflowers. As above, below, again. The brick wall is drawn in hard, double-thick black lines. Are the children inside the garden or outside?

The boy places his right foot inside the smaller of the two grass circles. The girl does the same, but reluctantly, toes first. The right side is not the heart side, right side first is first step wrong. The girl knows this, she leaves her left foot above the grass, her heart-side foot.

The girl is Worry, Caution; the boy, who plants his left foot down as firmly as a brick, damn the order of things, damn nature, is Unreliability, perhaps Panic.

These children will make no children. These children are hunters. The Reader cannot see their teeth.

The Tower is Trauma. A bolt of lightning strikes a stone fortress. A man in peasant leggings and a man in a gown fall, fall forever, face first, upside down. The Tower has three windows, flames erupt from each. The Tower has, or had, a coronet for a roof.

How easily a stone roof snaps off. One bolt of electricity, one bolt of charged dust, and off it comes. All around the Tower, the broken watch, is India-ink black.

Fall, a fall, to fall, falling. Gravity and demise. Two men knocked over.

Two men cannot make a child either.

The Ten of Cups is a consolation prize. Bounty, Love, Wine, Plenty. Fine wine and crystal. Lies, lies, lies.

I rub the card between my palms. I am wilful, was never a good listener.

Fuck the locked garden, fuck the rickety edifice. I want pleasure, more of more, an expertly poured champagne glass waterfall, all mine, and tall men in quality livery, hired-out handsomeness and giddy hours.

I want to have and I want to smash. Everything at once.

'Invisible?' Alexandar gently pushed my glasses back up on my nose. 'No, no. And so, I see you. You are here.'

'I was speaking poetically.'

'That is now big news.'

I shifted on the couch, taking my arm off Alexandar's shoulder. The spring sun, late for March, filled the open living room windows. Outside, a small gang of very small boys kicked a ball up and down the sidewalk in as disorderly a manner as possible, aiming for the broad cobbles of Willibald-Alexis-Strasse and its constant stream of fuming trucks. Berlin's children have no fear of cars.

Alexandar watched the brats with high Teutonic indifference. He rarely visited me in daylight hours. I had made him coffee and served him cake. Soon we would fuck.

'Berlin and Toronto are very different places,' I tried again. 'Berlin has its own obsessions, yes, and a big gay culture, of course, yes, so does Toronto, but Toronto has different ... needs. I can't meet those needs anymore.'

Alexandar crossed his legs and leaned into me. *Go on*, his face said, eyebrows up, *go on*.

'Okay, it's really very simple: I am forty-eight years old. I am overweight. I am not rich, I am not famous. I am not a "bear," I am not a "daddy." I don't belong anywhere in Toronto, and I'm about as coveted as an empty tin can. My time is finished there. I had my fun but I am past my prime. And even the stupidest gay man can see that, in seconds. Toronto trains gay men to weed out men like me. If I was rich or at least some sort of beloved aging artist, things would be different – but when men look at me now they don't see anything worth investing in, worth their time. I'm spent.

'I had fun while it lasted, but now I am supposed to do the decent and polite and dignified thing and just disappear, evaporate, go away. In Berlin, there are other rules, certainly, and I am starting to understand them, but in Berlin it is okay for me to be past thirty-five and still be sexual, to be fat and still be sexual, to be poor – everybody is poor here – and still be sexual, to be a nobody and still be sexual. Because in Berlin to not be sexual, right up until you die, is breaking the rules.

'I've seen men in their seventies fucking in the clubs here. It's wonderful. In Toronto, that would clear the room. In Toronto, there is still this British hangover about sex – sex is supposed to be discreet and only enjoyed by people who don't have more developed, more refined, interests.

'At my age and in my position, in Toronto, I am supposed to put my sex drive away and start collecting wine, or volunteer at a museum, or write a cranky restaurant column, or, best of all, move to a small town and have four dogs and maybe write a blog that nobody will ever read about local amateur theatre. It's too horrible. I can't go back to that. There is nothing to go back to.'

'And so, you are a refugee? Do you have a napkin? I will tie it over your hair. Just like the Syrian ladies.'

'You'll never understand.'

'Because what you saying is stupid.'

'No, it's the truth. What I am describing, the situation in Toronto, yes, yes, that is stupid. But I did not make it that way.'

'But you agree with this bad problem.'

'Agree with it? I feel … I'm angry. I don't … How can you say I agree with it?'

'You play a game, you agree with the rules, no? Why don't you just do whatever you want? Because you think inside your-self that these rules are true, heart true. You are arguing and then doing the things you are arguing, so you make a perfect circle. Around and around. You say, "I hate this game," and then you say, "Where is the starting line, I am going to run for this game now." Make your own game. Be a game. Kill the old game. The world is your lobster.'

'Oyster.'

Alexandar stood up and clapped his hands together. He closed the windows and drew the curtains. He pointed at the floor. I knew what that meant: *Be a dog.*

I got down on all fours. Alexandar stood over me, my head between his legs. He squeezed my neck until I saw bright spots, flaring patches of cobalt blue. I smelled lilacs. Or thought I did.

'Good boy,' Alexandar coached. 'Good boy.' He smacked my rump. 'Lots of good fleisch here,' he chuckled. He grabbed the low, drooping bag of my belly, took a handful of fat and dug in with his fingers. 'And so, here. Enough for everyone.' He straightened up, shook his legs, unbuttoned his fly, and pulled my head up by the ears. 'Good, yes, good, yes,' he said.

I went to work.

Alexandar was always chatty while I sucked his cock, rumi-native. Once, I was told a very detailed story about the family that escaped East Berlin by hooking a zip line from a tall building and sliding down to freedom. Alexandar knew the width of the cable, the design of the harness, how much the oldest child weighed. If he could find someone to blow him from under a desk, he'd make a great chat-show host.

I puffed away while he talked, my spit tinkling onto the rented carpet.

'The old Germans, the simple ages ones, how do you say it? The ones before Jesus? The first Germans. They didn't like virgins. That is a movie story, Hollywood. The virgins and the big rock and the knives. Sacrifice.

'Yes, of course they did this, and they burned people for their gods, but it is a lie that only virgins could go to the gods. The old Germans, the true Germans, they took the old people and the whores and the women with ten children and the men with five wives, they put a knife in the people who had lived, who had knowledge, who were not innocent and not stupid. Men who made murders, women who buried their own babies. Useful people.

'The gods did not want virgins. Virgins are empty bowls. The gods want meat.'

New sounds, for spring. Underneath the bed, a bell tinkles, a wee bell, a bell perhaps the size of a penny, a shirt button. I have never seen it, of course. *Jingle, jingle, jingle*, it goes, whenever Alexandar is asleep, whenever I am not asleep. And rain sounds, on blue-sky days. The patter and splat of rain hitting a car hood, of rain bouncing on a tin café table, of rain pinging, half ice and half water, on a thin windowpane. And the *click-click-click* of an adding machine being vigorously employed, but as if underneath a glass bell jar, or from a short distance (this is the sound that accompanies Alexandar when he eats, and, yes, I have asked him about his teeth, his teeth are good as diamonds). The scratch of a wooden match being struck every time I piss. The thunder of a log rolling down a hill whenever I write a letter. Never music. Never harmony, never chords and counter-chords, never rhythm. Sounds out of order, or sounds in an order of their own making. Sounds insensible, or primordial, of the swamps and ponds, of the mud. Sounds before the invention of humanity, of beauty (or ugliness), sounds uninformed, from the time before culture. Sounds hardly unique to the trained ear. The ears of voles, or chickadees, or the ever-watching jackdaws. All insects.

And Berlin in spring is all noise. With each temperature increase, each degree upward, the number of people on the street increases twofold. Berliners would lie down on the street, the middle of the road, drink a beer, and read the paper under the traffic, as long as the sun was shining. Berliners cannot stop talking when the sun is shining. The city indulges itself, enjoys a three-month manic episode, as only a winter city can. The sun is reluctant to set, it inches backward slowly, like a beloved king retreating from a balcony, a king addicted to roses and garlands, the cheers of house maids and cab drivers, the adoration of the boisterous class. The parks are full, the beer halls are full, the shops are full. Every stomach pops out a little, stuffed with lamb and white asparagus, every eye is watery, beer-sparkled.

Alexandar insists we do everything outdoors: eat and drink, easy enough, kiss, put our hands into each other's open flies, watch movies on my laptop in my courtyard, walk for hours. Tempelhofer Feld is his favourite walk. We always take the same route. Enter through the south gate, move to the centre of the park, the wide, grassy stretch between the abandoned landing strips, then turn north, into the trees: a path in the shape of a Y, minus the left prong. Every time. Once I suggested we turn east, or west, and Alexandar turned on me, nostrils flaring. 'Why?' he asked, spitting. 'Why?' I muttered something about making a nice change, something about bears going over the mountain, made a bad metaphor about change and rest, winced. Alexandar marched forward, true to his own plans. I followed. I always followed. Together we tramped down the same grass, made lines in the mud true as runes. I was so in love.

I hate that park. It tries too hard to be ghostly, to be a second world, a ruin, an aerial Atlantis. Tempelhofer Feld rises up from a flat, dull stretch of Columbiadamm, hanging, dismissive, over a low, watery patch of plain scrub, a half-forest crabbed with dead leaves and untamed vines, a pecking ground for mud birds and Berlin's trailer dwellers (who are, too bad for romance, not Roma, not tinkerers, who make no midnight fires and don't bang on concertinas). Tempelhofer Feld is a mound, flat at the top, like a Celtic burial knoll, or a butte, only larger, much larger. Tempelhofer Feld is Berlin's anchor, an egg-shaped weight of land, a mole on a cheek. The Knights Templar, the cleverest men in history, used it for their satanic sacrifices. They knew what they were doing – Tempelhofer is a vast plate with a deep centre, a raised platform with a low, liquid-catching pool in its dead centre, a blood basin. The Nazis were so stupid – they flattened and paved the very grounds under which they would most likely have found all the magic knives and swords and crowns and amulets their rulers sent men all the way to Tibet to (not) find. Even now, well past the last great outbreak of Teutonic devil worship, I know. I know this is where Alexandar will bring me, sure as moonlight and under moonlight, to feed me to the Viy. Alexandar is marking the ground with his sacrifice's feet, my fat feet. Alexandar is preparing the altar, waiting for the June bugs and the beetles, the grasshoppers and the mealworms to fatten and dig their way out of the grass roots, lustful and hungry, antennae sharp as nettle leaves. Every step we take together is another sharpening of the altar knife.

Before they steamrolled Tempelhofer to make way for landing strips, the Nazis buried an enormous magnet under the spot where, according to their official spiritualists, Jews all, the Knights Templar held court. A magnet the size of a summer house. To the Nazi bureaucracy, this was a folly to be tolerated – expensive, yes, but what wasn't expensive? To the true believers, devotees of Tesla to the man, the magnet would draw all the scattered mystical ions, the centuries of lost blood power, to one sacred and indestructible spot. The process would take fifty years, as earth is slow to give up its charms, slow as a

Viennese waitress. But fifty years is nothing in a thousand-year plan. No government since the Reich has had the courage, or the money, to dig up the magnet. Alexandar shows me exactly where it is every time we walk through the park. 'Here,' he says, 'here. Take off your shoes,' he says. 'Lie down,' he says. And I do. At the back of my head, through my skull, I hear – no, I feel – the sound of water splashing against wrought iron, and, seconds after, a blade scraped up and down a strop.

I trawled the sex clubs. I was not of this world. I was half-awake, day and night. I was twitchy and fretful and sluggish and reluctant, all at once. I felt trapped inside and I left my apartment every day. I was catty and sullen and chatty and generous. I spent freely and carefully saved all my coins in a tin cookie box. I told my secrets to strangers and I made up a new history for myself.

The men I met were in much the same state as me – horny but bored, fed up but too poor to travel, stupid but aware, in love with somebody who was not in the room. Somebody who would never be in the room.

Alexandar phoned. Behind his voice I heard other men, a lot of laughing, and what sounded like a string ensemble, if string ensembles used metal twine.

'Come now,' Alexandar barked. 'Come now fun everyone fun come.' He rattled off an address in Hermannplatz. A Croatian restaurant. *Maybe,* I thought, *maybe Alexandar is Croatian?* Mystery solved. One of many, so many. Berlin is packed with Croats, but you'd never know it. Refugees and gangsters and illegal migrants and war criminals and the poor have so much to hide.

The restaurant was jammed with burly, hairy men. The only woman was an elderly waitress who took great pleasure in swatting her customers with whatever came to hand: a menu, a dish towel, a plate, a disabled man's walking stick. Everyone was shouting drunk. The restaurant was simply called Croatian Restaurant. Refugees dislike complications and distrust niceties. Refugees thrive in the ad hoc, the temporary, the slapped together. Nobody in the restaurant spoke a word of German, or English. Alexandar led me around, introducing me to Gorans and Sadkos and Razzos and Radeks.

'And you like here, yes?'

'All the men have moustaches. I feel like I'm in the Ottoman cavalry.'

'Hmmm. Things not to say, okay?'

'I'll behave.'

'Drink. Behave bad. Don't speak.'

Within an hour I was head-bobbing drunk. Alexandar poured thimble after thimble of a pale white liquid, a drink that looked like melted moonstone. 'It is made of the tall grass,' he said. 'And it is made of the trees,' he said. After every shot downed, more men joined us at our table. I was surrounded. I liked the way the men smelled, of pine and carbolic soap, of rosewater and wood varnish, ball sweat and armpit sweat and paraffin. I wanted to bear-hug them all, and then get under the table and work my way around. These were not men, they were stags with shoes, elk in silk shirts, grizzlies in faded jeans.

Alexandar slung his arm over my shoulder and told the yelling men something I didn't understand. I heard 'Kanada' and 'Martin' and what sounded like 'darling' but I knew could not be anything so feminine. The men nodded at me appreciatively, as if I'd invented penicillin. Or was rich. I caught a greedy, lupine look in their eyes. The under-the-table fantasy suddenly seemed very possible. The muscles under my balls tightened. The man opposite Alexandar, a great monster of a man with forearms the width of a coffee table, smiled at Alexandar the way one farmer smiles at another over the fall harvest, over the grain-fattened calves. Alexandar ruffled my hair. More drinks came, then more. My eyes rolled up to the top of my head and stayed there. Everybody laughed.

'They are liking you!' Alexandar shouted. It was a shouting sort of restaurant. And a restaurant entirely without food, as far as I could tell.

The waitress hovered over the table long enough to empty out the tin ashtrays and stare at my dumbfounded face. She beaned me with a spent butt. 'You talk too much,' she spat.

Alexandar laughed and gave her a euro.

'Who are these people?' I asked.

'My good friends of so many years and times together over good and bad but now mostly good.'

'They're very friendly.'

'Yes, but not forever. They like new toys.'

'Toys? Toys?'

'Boys. Boys.'

Alexandar put his mouth to my ear. 'This one,' he said, 'with big arms, you watch him soon he will try to pick you up.'

'But I'm with you,' I said.

'No, see, no. Pick up. Like a box. Off the ground. He is a show-off. Strong as winter.'

'Fun!' I slurred.

'Yes, but … '

I leaned into the man with the ox-yoke forearms. 'Lift me,' I shouted. He laughed, shook his head, shrugged. I tried to stand up, do a charade of lifting a crate. Ox-yoke-arms laughed again and pushed me back into my chair with one finger. 'Lift me,' I shouted. 'C'mon, lift me!'

Alexandar slapped me hard on the back of the head.

I could still feel the sting of his palm when I woke up. My face was flat on the table, my glasses had been taken off and gently folded into my shirt pocket. My cheeks were sticky with sweet-smelling liquor. I felt delighted and horny and sick to my stomach. I watched the men around me with one eye half-open, pretending to be passed out. I'm a sneaky drunk.

The men were much quieter now. I heard Alexandar murmuring what sounded like a poem, a chant. When he was silent, the men murmured back at him, repeating the syllables. Call and response, response and call. The room reeked of piss and snuffed candles, beery vomit.

I felt one hand touch my back, then another, then a dozen. The touch of each hand was light, hovering, electric. Butterfly-tense. The chanting grew fainter. I opened my eye wide and saw a man, a new member to the group, staring at me but not seeing me. His face was red and hot, as if he'd been running, or fighting. His hand was on my back too. His arms were bare and hairy, spotted with geometric, ash-black tattoos, prison tattoos. I looked around some more. The man's shirt was off and his chest was smeared with gore, raw meat and blood, offal. His torso quivered. He was beautiful. His chest hair swirled around his pectorals and shoulders like a hurricane. I wiggled an eyebrow at him. Nothing. He was in a trance.

The hands on my back suddenly moved as one, toward my head, lifting my shirt off my back until it was wrapped around my shoulders and covered my face. The chanting stopped. Alexandar spoke, barking out a simple order in a language I had never heard him speak. The words were full of L sounds, short L's and long L's. The other men removed their hands. I felt a tongue run up my spine. I flinched. The effort made me light-headed. I began to see dark wrinkles in the corners of my eyes. My ears were warm and there was not enough air under my shirt.

Before I passed out again, I felt heavy objects being placed on my back. A wet plate just behind my neck, followed by a long, flat piece of cold metal aligned with my vertebrae, then another, shorter flat of metal running horizontally across my lower back, just above my ass. The room was still and silent. I heard, then felt, long, slow breaths, acidic streams of air that curled around my ears, between my belly and the table, little breezes that tickled my rib cage and the hair between my shoulder blades.

One of the men, I don't know which, laid his forearm on top of the large metal plank. The hairs above his elbow, thick as thread, reached, static-charged, for my pale skin. I heard a sharp intake of breath, a hissing sound. A first drop landed on my spine, then another, then a stream. The liquid was hot and thick and smelled like a box of nails, like crushed cloves. The liquid ran down my sides and pooled in my lap. The men began to breathe again, in unison, a kind of panting, huffing breath, and I went away, into the blank dark.

Three days after Alexandar's weird ceremony, the bleeding started. First, the fingertips on my left hand. Little droplets that pulsed and bubbled until they formed streams. I wrapped my hand in a tea towel, but the bleeding only grew stronger. I could not find the source, the wound. I washed the blood off under the kitchen faucet and the pinkish stream moved counter to the flow of the tap water, against the tide, and stilled inches above the drain. The blood and water mixed and remixed, forming shapes. The face of a goat. A large eye inside the outline of a kidney. Flowers that budded and bloomed and wilted in seconds. Flames. A goat again, with one horn.

Just as quickly as it started, the bleeding stopped. I lay down on the sofa and waited for my vision to stop tilting, for my head to clear. I felt a cool sensation in my groin. Cool as mint toothpaste, and then sticky wet. I stood up and peeled off my pants. My balls were dappled in tiny red dots, pinpricks of fresh, full, devil's-tail-red blood. I ran to the bathroom and sat in the empty tub. The blood trickled out of me in hot bubbles. My balls were gooey, the blood began to crust over. Underneath my legs, the mess congealed, grew shiny and hard as nail polish. A horn took shape, then a second. The goat. The goat with three eyes.

I stood up and showered, scrubbing my body with stinging soap. The blood came again, from both hands and my balls and my forehead. I stood under the shower for half an hour, until all the blood was gone, sluiced away. Patterns emerged in the steam. Animal tails, thorns on stems, ivy, miles of ivy, chains of horrid, blown-out flowers, a hundred tiny spoiled things, broken things, little evils, ants and teeth and the points of daggers.

I am out of my mind, I said out loud. And then I laughed. *Utterly out of my mind. Finally. How ideal, how refreshing, to let go. I will have visions and not be afraid. I will be unclean and do the unclean. I will jump up and down on graves and not be afraid. I will walk into traffic. I will call on the dead and the never-alive. I will be insane and be very good at being insane. I am no longer bound by pretty lies and colourful rules. I am free and spinny as a pinwheel.*

Later, Alexandar brought me dinner. Poached fish and pickled potatoes, with white beer. Disgusting. I ate like an ape, paws straight into the muck. Alexandar hardly noticed. He ate with a knife. He always ate with a knife, sailor-style.

'Who were those men? The men at the restaurant?'

'This men are men friends. That is all.'

'Tell me everything.'

'And what is the telling? You meet a guy and he is your friend or not. And he is your friend so you drink with him. And so. Don't be so American, with complications for water and air, questions for the sky and the sun.'

'Don't be so Euro– What are you anyway? Croatian? Russian? Not German.'

'You see and so you do it again. I am Alexandar and I brought you good fish to eat and already the beer is gone. Nothing to speak more.'

'I think you're a gangster. Or the Devil. Or both. '

Alexandar laughed, laughed deeply, from his belly. He pinched my chin. 'The Devil is here.' He squeezed my jaw, hard. 'And the Devil is here,' he said, twisting my head toward his face. 'And the Devil is very true here,' he whispered while he rubbed my stomach, his hands warm as wool. 'Here. Here. Very here.' He kissed me gently, like a shy teen. In a moment, he was on top of me. He pressed his excited cock against my chest. In a moment, his cock was in my mouth. In another moment, he came in my throat, spilling seed down my chin.

I swallowed all that I could and licked off the rest.

'And so ask me another question,' he teased.

'I want something of yours.'

'I am just giving you a whole mouth – '

'No', I interrupted, 'something to keep.'

'Sometimes I am thinking you are a woman.'

I stared at Alexandar until he shrugged and let out a long sigh. The tables were turning. This was the first nudge.

Alexandar dug his wallet out of his front pocket (kept there, he always reminded me, because Berlin is full of pickpockets) and scrounged through the wad of receipts and euros and old S-Train tickets. 'Ah! And here! Put a candle under it and also flowers. Saint Alexandar.' He handed me a photograph, a small photograph only twice as large as a postage stamp. The edges were scalloped. The photo was black and white.

Alexandar as a young man, maybe twenty-five. Alexandar as a young man dressed in a uniform, a uniform with a high collar and two silvery buttons at the chest. Alexandar, young and crisp, hair cut short, holding an upright Brownie camera in front of a mirror, a mirror split in two, one side facing left, one right. Two Alexandars. Handsome as sin.

'Now,' I said out loud, 'now I have so many Alexandars.' The Alexandar who snored beside me in bed and borrowed my shirts. The Alexandar who would not tell me where he came from or the names of his parents. The Alexandar with mysterious friends. The Alexandar of the past, the man who took this photograph. Plus, the twin Alexandars in the photograph, identical men who did not, not quite, appear to be the same man.

And then, not in my hand, the Alexandars never to be seen, the Alexandars in the photograph that Alexandar kept, that only Alexandar knew, the unquestionable picture of Alexandar photographing Alexandar meeting Alexandar. The photograph of the three Alexandars, a harmonious triangle, all points equal. The photograph that swallowed the man in my bed, years ago, years before I came along (but I know I was expected). The photograph that bound him, binds him still, for life and long, long after. The photograph that was perfection, unattainable earthly perfection, purchased at such a high price.

What I held in my hand was a replica of a moment before a promise was made, a moment before a greater, more eternal moment, one that lasts to this day – the moment before an exquisite deal was struck, just before Alexandar's hand touched the thorny palm of the beast. Somewhere, close to his heart, Alexandar kept a second but true, razor-true, photograph, a vision of the three Alexandars posed in simple mockery of the Holy Trinity.

I will never see this binding spell, but I hardly needed to. What I held in my hand was the stumbling first try. How sweet, how laughable. In a safe and foul place, the man I was in love with stored the contract, blazed onto celluloid, the smile and click and flash and aperture wink that both made Alexandar and forever contains Alexandar. The photograph, true and lasting, that is Alexandar's deal with the Devil.

What I held in my hand was not a warning, it was an offering. I accepted.

There was one thing about Alexandar, not a big enough thing to stop seeing him over, but still … He could never accept responsibility for anything. One night he dropped a wineglass on the kitchen floor and I cleaned it up because, according to him, it was my fault for not drying the glasses properly after I washed them. It was defensive and even bullish on his part, but that is the default German response to any situation: someone else is to blame. There is a defect in the German character that prevents them from accepting any sort of blame or responsibility. Obviously, there are historical precedents for this. But the war is only the biggest, lumbering example. I got rammed right in the kneecap by this woman pushing a stroller and she scolded me for being in the way. She was pushing her brat and talking on the phone at the same time and crashing into everything in front of her, and each time she banged into something she cursed that thing for being in her way, as if the material world was meant to bend to her needs, not the other way around. Now imagine a whole city, a whole country, full of like-minded people. The concept of fault, even in the most simple situations, in cut-and-dried accidents where one party is clearly in the wrong, is always up for negotiation and 99 per cent of the time up for outright denial. I have never heard a German say, 'I'm sorry, that was my mistake.'

Alexandar behaved this way all the time, and I was not even certain he was 'full German,' as they like to say here. He behaved this way in bed, with his body. If he was fucking me and I got a leg cramp and I needed to pause, he would keep on sawing away, not because he didn't give a crap about my discomfort, but because in order for him to stop a moment he would have to tell himself that as the 'top' he positioned me in the unsustainable configuration, and, therefore, might need to fix the way our bodies are hinged together. One night I was belly down on the bed and he was inside me, nice enough, but then he spread my legs apart a little farther and held my ankles up over my back, and my inner left thigh felt like it was being stabbed with a dull pike. I made a *hold on* kind of grunt, and I know he heard me, but on he went, deeper and with more force. I looked over my shoulder and he shrugged, to say, *well, fix it*, all the while pinching my ankles farther backwards, into my shoulders. Now, I knew Alexandar was a sadist. But in a fun way, not a neurotic way. In his mind, anything he did or did not do is irrelevant in the immediate moment. All that was relevant was his need to carry on.

I took Alexandar to a Walpurgisnacht party. Walpurgisnacht is an old Germanic-pagan holiday, set on the night before May Day. It's like Halloween without the costumes or candy (or, too bad, the pumpkins) – the idea being that the night is exactly six months before Halloween and, like Halloween/All Saints' Day, is a night when the world of the dead and the world of the living are very close together, each visible to the other. Black witches are said to meet on mountaintops where they dance and drink and make jolly with Satan. Or, for white witches, dance and drink and perform rituals to make the next half of the year better and to offer blessings. The party I was at was a bit of both, grey magic.

Berlin queers are a funny lot. They can't get anywhere on time and can't organize the simplest of expeditions or host a dinner party before midnight, and if you take their mobile phones away, you might as well cut off their legs and dig out their eyes. But declare something a 'ritual,' which comes, always, with the unspoken promise of a potential orgy, and they arrive early, which is unheard of, and with drinks and snacks, also unheard of.

We met up with my little queer family at the bottom of Hasenheide Park. Berlin is basically a chain of parks with some bits of city in between. Alexandar was horrified, he always is when he meets my friends. I sometimes wonder how he was raised. His face takes on this half-stunned, half-aggravated look, like he's watching a house fire. I am being polite: he hates my friends. 'Which one is also the one who is male and plus female too?' Or, 'Who again is the big one with the tits and the Minnie Mouse haircut but is not smart and sings?' Or, my all-time fave, 'Why your friends are not made correct?' Like most northern Europeans, Alexandar finds diversity challenging.

Hasenheide Park is built all around a small hill – small by Canadian standards. Cobbled trails lead all the way to the top of the 'mountain,' as they call it here. It's romantic and sweet, lined with horse chestnut and flowering trees with white tufts of honey-scented petals. Noisy birds hop from tree to tree, trilling and squealing. I'm told the park is overrun with foxes, but I've never seen one. I held Alexandar's hand. I caught a few glances from the others. Alexandar is sexy but he is not an overtly sexual person, or, rather, he does not display his sexuality well or explicitly. How to put it? Standing next to a cluster of trans people, queers, and artist freaks, he looks like a cop.

That's probably why I'm attracted to him in the first place. I live in a community of limitless openness. A discreet man, a man who blends in, is a puzzle to me, a curiosity, candy inside a plain egg.

Our little troupe made it to the top of the hill just before 11:00 p.m. Everybody had a task: spread the blanket on the ground, assemble the candles in a circle, find wood for the bonfire, make a coven circle on the ground with salt and red yarn, pour the wine. We started with a toast of schnapps: *To Summer and the West Wind*. Then we formed a tight circle with our bodies, and each person took a length of red yarn off the ground and tied it around their right wrist. Another toast: *We Are Bound*. Alexandar became very still. He was either mortified or enthralled.

A pad of paper was passed around, and L, the head witch, instructed us to each take a piece and write, backwards, the word that best described an attribute or a bad habit or a nuisance or even an enemy that needed to be gone. Everyone took their time. Alexandar wrote something down and then scratched it out and then wrote another word and scratched it out and then another. Does that mess up the magic?

L set a pair of scissors in the centre of the salt circle. *When you feel ready to 'let go,'* we were told, *take up the scissors and cut yourself free, then use the dangling yarn to bind the sheet of paper naming that which you least desire, tie the yarn tight, whisper the word on the paper to yourself three times, and toss the bundle into the bonfire*. Some in the circle performed the ceremony instantly, as if they were holding hot rocks they wanted out of their hands. Some took over an hour to unburden themselves. I gave myself a few minutes, enjoyed some long breaths, and then got on with it. My word was *envy* (I'm probably not supposed to tell). The paper gave off a frying-bacon sound when it hit the bonfire.

Alexandar stayed quiet. I wondered if maybe the situation was too much for him, too queer and maybe even too women-centred (he never talks about women, female friends, sisters, nothing). I watched him, stood a little back to get a better view. Underneath his feet the dirt was smudged, flattened out, tamped down. He was rocking on the balls of his feet, gently but firmly. I watched his calf muscles swell and deflate. His pants were tight as shrink wrap. By the time half the circle had tossed their cares into the fire, Alexandar was dancing in place, toes pressed into the ground, heels raised. He was straining. I didn't look at his face.

A woman I had only met an hour before started to ask me about Canada, to make small talk, when I felt a tug on my wrist. Alexandar was pulling on his side of the yarn. He pulled until it snapped. Then he snapped off the other side. The person attached to him, my friend B, stared at Alexandar for a moment, then turned away, embarrassed. Alexandar carefully wound up his bit of paper, spat on the ground, then rapidly unwound the bundle and stuffed the snarled clump of yarn into his coat pocket. Without so much as a nod, he walked away, straight down the hill path, into the dark.

I didn't know what to do. Chase after him? Let him go? Why did he leave? I guess this was a classic relationship dilemma unfolding – were Alexandar and I at the fraught *go after him* stage or the resigned *don't take the drama bait* stage? I was too stunned to decide. Weirdly, nobody noticed he was gone. Blame the night air, and the pot.

When I got home, Alexandar was waiting for me on the couch. I don't remember ever making keys for him, but I must have done.

'Where did you go?' I asked him.

'I am here, and so you see.'

'Okay, yes. Why did you go?'

Alexandar shrugged. I knew by then what that shrug meant: *no more talking*. So, we fucked instead. That man was born to fuck, I'll give him that. Where do some people get all their energy?

Contents of personal belongings, patient # 29873, Martin Murray Heather. Coat pocket, left side.

– 1 standard 5×7 piece of notepad paper. No watermark. Paper off-white. Paper rolled to form a scroll. Paper smudged with dirt. Red fibres visible on one side of paper. Paper blank on outer side of scroll. Inner side contained the following indecipherable text:

e s a e l e r

– 1 postcard, FIFA World Cup souvenir. Blasko Dragonovic, centre field position, Team Serbia. Verso: the word 'khlystys' in black ink, illustrations of flowers in black ink, apparently decorating the text; 3 illustrations of hammers, all crudely drawn. Inconclusive match to Patient's handwriting.

[n.b. 'khlystys': pre-modern Russian word for 'whip'; may also refer to 17th-century obscure cult of radical antinomians who believed the path to salvation was through extreme sin, also known as the 'left-handed path,' but Patient appears to have, or chooses not to reveal, any knowledge of this sect]

Once a year, the warden visits. He announces new programs, new initiatives, new 'strategies for holisticizing care and delivering the best post-judicial process experience for all our clients and visiting self-admittees.' I am the only one listening, always. I find him adorable, the warden. He is literally full of hope. How exhausting for him.

Once a year, after the warden visits, our rooms are repainted. I am scolded, calmly, for scratching the walls, told I am not hurting anyone or anything but myself. Truly, my nails are a sight, little more than stubs, frayed at the ends, raw in the corners. I rather enjoy the scolding. Contact is contact.

For weeks now I have been trying to remember the spelling of a single word. A word I received on a card (weirdly, a card depicting a Serbian football player, who was, in my view, a bit wolf-faced), a postcard, with one hastily scrawled word : K, H, L, Y ... and then either an S or another L or a T or a Y. Now that I have a fresh wall, and, again and forever, all the time imaginable, I can try to sort out the word in my head. Khly ... stl. Khly ... tysl. Khly ... tlysl. The combinations are limitless, mathematically impossible to ever know.

When my food is brought, I shout out the latest version of this magic word, the one I am most sure of that day. So far, no response. I'm in this for the long haul. One day, a guard will pause, breathe in quickly when I say the magic word, or puff out a snort, or even laugh, and then I will know. I will know the word. But the word will not set me free. I've never been that kind of writer, only that kind of killer, the itchy-trigger type.

The card marked with the magic word was wedged under my doorknob, between the metal and the door, and rather roughly, its bottom side bent and torn. As if done in a hurry. This being Berlin, I assumed it was another angry note about noise or smells or just my general foreignness – Berliners are chronic note-leavers. Unsigned notes. But when I turned it over, away from the glaring Serbian sportsman, there was only the one word, that damned word I can't recall. The word was encircled with little black flowers, daisy-shaped, all hand-drawn (badly), little black flowers and, in the far top left corner, three tiny drawings of hammers, common toolbox hammers.

Flowers and hammers. So Soviet, old Europe, violence and blessings, black pagan formulas, black arts. I taped the card over my mirror, Serbian snarl facing outward, facing me. *Let it come down*, I thought. *Let it come down, hammer and black blooms.*

Alexandar gave the card a sideways glance. He had just sat me down in the tub, fully dressed, and was unzipping his jeans, hoisting himself up to piss on me, when he saw the dog-man footballer.

'Volos,' he said.

'Is that like *Cheers* just before you splash all over me?'

'Have the respect!' Alexandar pissed on my head. 'The old gods, to them, gifts.' He drenched my shirt, my legs. 'And where you found this boy? Sport boy? He looks a priest.' Alexandar ran out of piss, shook the last drops across my face. 'Volos. Old god. Eats boys and priests. Virgins also yes.'

'Then I have nothing to worry about.'

Alexandar twisted my ear. 'Stupid and virgin is same.'

Until the walls and the floors and the ceiling are filled with my pecks and peels, I will know this word. I will bleed for this word. This word is a lantern. Pity it is not a key.

Statement by Martin Murray Heather. Transcribed and countersigned by Polizeihauptkommissar Rörig and Polizeioberkommissar Offmann, Polizeidirektion 4 Südwest, Eiswaldtstrasse 18, 12249 Berlin.

Martin Murray Heather: I want you to understand that nothing I did to Alexandar was hard for me. I know I am supposed to say that I am confused and sad and don't remember what really happened and don't know why I killed him. But that is not true. I knew exactly what I was doing and I was happy to kill him. He killed me first. No, that's not true either. We killed each other. He just died first.

Do you know where Hels Pfuhl is? The park, in Alboinplatz? Of course you do, yes, I'm sorry. You found his body there. Do you know what kind of place it is? The history? People swim there now. In the little lake. Where they used to throw the bodies. They? The pagans, your ancestors. The people before Christ. The Franks, the Vandals, the old knights, and the famous ones too. Your beloved Templars. Bastards, the lot of them. Handsome bastards too, I bet. Like you two.

Before God, there were gods. Hundreds. The people who lived here went to the lake and made magic circles with stones and burning bushes and their bodies. Someone was chosen, usually the very old or the very sick, and they agreed to death, for the good of the rest of the village, for their families. Their bodies were pulled apart, head first, then arms and legs, and then genitals last, dug out with forks. Then the body parts were burned in the centre of the circle. The bones were distributed to the priests first, and the family would get a rib or a finger bone. It was very organized and very clean. The ashes were given to the lake, because the lake gave life. And life needs death or it is not life, it is just … movement and breathing and shitting. Nothing. Look at you two, you're staring at me like I'm out of my mind, but what do you do every day, how do you bring home money for food and heat and shoes? You need people to die for you to live.

Yes, yes, I'm getting to that. Do you have a train to catch? Is there a more important body by another lake somewhere? Don't rush me. I will not be rushed. I will not. I've met a lot of men like you two in my life, men who are always asking for the truth. You all have one thing in common: you don't know how to listen.

Alexandar picked me up around 10:00 p.m., yes, ten at night, 22:00. Whatever. Ten, maybe a bit after, but not much. He was never late. He came inside and waited for me. He sat in the chair he liked the most, we called it his chair. Sometimes he made me sit on the floor beside him, like a pet. I liked it. Forget that, you would not understand. He came in, he looked around and said my place smelled good, smelled clean, and he sat down and waited for me to find my coat. He liked my apartment, he called it my little bougie sitting room. I guess it is bougie. I'm bougie. Most killers are, we're ordinary.

I got my coat and we went out. I think we kissed a bit in the lobby. No, I know we did. A good, deep kiss. And then another. Don't make that face, please, or I will stop talking. Yes, yes you did. Your little curled lips. What a prissy little housewife you would make. Off to Mass with your best shoes and a purse full of tissues. Fuck off.

[Tape is silent for 4 minutes.]

If you stop smoking, I'll finish the story.

[Tape is silent for 36 seconds.]

We got on the U6 to Kaiserin-Augusta-Strasse and walked over to Alboinplatz. We didn't say much. What does anybody talk about on a walk to a park on a summer night? You talk about the summer, how lovely it is. You talk about the air, the sweet air. If you think we had an argument, you're off track. God, are all your murders that simple? Nice job. Nice job you've got there.

We walked and we held hands under the trees. The park was empty. I thought it was. Alexandar said, 'Let's go to the lake.' Honestly, I thought we were going to fuck in the park. And I was worried we'd get arrested! Ha! You'd be deporting me now, wouldn't you? Or is that too low for you, deporting Canadians? I guess so. You guys are the murder men. Big jobs.

No, I am not being disrespectful. Germans have no sense of humour. Canadians like to tease, okay? It's how we get along with each other. It's why everybody loves us so much. When we're not killing their citizens.

There were other men at the lake. Eight or ten other men. A couple of them looked familiar, I met them once at a bar, friends of Alexandar's, but not friendly, if you know what I mean. I don't know if Alexandar really had friends. He just had men around him. I used to think they worked for him, or he worked for them. I never figured it out. It hardly matters now. No, I can't tell you their names. No, I can't look at pictures. I can't tell you anything about them. It was dark and they were careful. No eye contact.

These men, they moved … they moved like foxes, low to the ground, heads up, alert. Fast but quiet. No tracks in the grass, not a bent leaf. I could smell their breath, cigarettes and vodka, but I couldn't see what they were doing, the plan, the pattern, until I did. A triangle, a simple triangle. The tallest man at the top of the pyramid, the shortest men along the base. Me in the middle, Alexandar behind me, still as a tree trunk.

Alexandar told me to spread my legs apart. I thought it was a game, a sex game. I've done worse, worse than a dozen guys at once. Oh, there's that look again. You fucking asked, so now you fucking know.

[Tape is paused here, detectives leave the room, MMH is heard whispering but the words are undetectable, 11 minutes pass according to Inspector's time stamp.]

Back for more? Did you have to go call your girlfriends? Get an itch? Stupid, stupid cunts.

Yes, I will continue to be abusive! You want to know the whole story but you act like fourteen-year-old boys when the details get rough. Which is it?

Fine. Leave me alone like that again and I will never speak again. I mean that. Never. No words. Do you like open cases? I thought not.

Alexandar told me to spread my legs. I thought it was a game. I did what he asked. I always did. I'm that kind of lover. Alexandar came up behind me and put his foot – let me figure, I was standing this way, so – his left foot on the ground between my legs. He put his hands on my shoulders and jerked me backwards, yes, like that, straight back, and I was off balance, I was caught against his body. He used his right foot for balance, hmm, yes, like that, like an easel. I was almost bent over backwards against him. He was very strong, remember, very strong.

[MMH cries for 3 minutes here, tape is silent.]

He held me backwards and the other men came closer. They were singing, a low song. I didn't understand the language. It was not German, it sounded more like Russian but I don't know, not as harsh as Russian, more L sounds and more S sounds … No, not Turkish either. Yes, sure, I can try, we can try that later. Is he cute, your Russian detective? I don't know the song, the melody was not, was not a melody. Does that make sense? It was sung words but not a song, not a proper song, not musical. Maybe chanting, maybe, but really bad chanting! I don't know. It felt like a church prayer but all the words and sounds were backwards. Yes, yes, I will try to remember more.

They kept coming closer. Really, I still thought it was a game. I thought Alexandar would shove me to the ground and I would have to suck all these guys off. We used to do that practically once a week, go to some bar and I'd suck off the guys Alexandar picked. No, I loved it. Loved it. Yeah, well, sometimes it's fun to be a dog. Where? In what bars can't that happen? Do you even live in Berlin? God, you're hopeless. Don't you know any fags at all? Oh, 'not that kind.' Hmmm. I feel sorry for them, your fags. Yes, that's true. I'm the one in prison now.

Basically, they surrounded me. One man right in front of my face, the one at the top of the pyramid, the tallest one – no, I told you, no eye contact – two guys on each side of me, and, I think, six or seven guys in the back, behind Alexandar. We were pressed together. One of them wore too much cologne, one of the guys on the – wait a sec, I was this way – on the right of me. I don't know, all perfume smells the same to me, flowers and tree bark and charcoal, something cheap. Off the rack. Sure, of course. You have a perfume bank? Germans think of everything. Bring me something pretty from the stockroom.

We were a perfect triangle. All of our bodies, tight, together. They stopped singing, or praying, whatever it was. We stood there for the longest time. It seemed long to me. I could see the stars over my head and the tops of trees and Alexandar's forearms and a tall man, just his forehead. I was hot, too warm. All those bodies. Yes, I was excited. 'Excited' – so cute. I had a hard-on, if that's what you are, of course, asking. Like you wouldn't if your dick was pressed against ten women. C'mon. It was beautiful, yes, that's the exact word, beautiful. Men together can be beautiful, even ugly men. There is a grace when men move together, the way they are cautious and careless at the same time, all that tension in the hands, in the stomach, between cocks that touch by accident. I don't know how to explain this to you … Do you play soccer? Football, okay, same thing. Foosball. You know what I mean then, that animal perfection, moving without thinking about moving. Exactly.

And then the whole … The moment changed. I don't know.

No, I do know. I do know, I know precisely. They turned on me. Our bodies were not warm together anymore. A chill ran through us, lightning chills. The wind came up and the trees were rustling and … it got violent. The tall man turned his back to me. He barked out something, a word, it sounded like 'tylsen' or 'silan' or … It was not a word, maybe a kind of yell, a cheer, but low, so low, a noise from a barrel. The other men turned their backs on me too, on both of us, Alexandar and me, and then, then, they started fighting. Really fighting. Hitting each other, punching and kicking and ... one man put his fist into another man's eye and there was blood pouring out of his eye and down his face ... I saw another man kick a smaller man in the guts – no, not kick, but dig, he was trying to dig out the man's guts with the toe of his boot. And there was cheering, they were all cheering, wolf whistles – you know [tape records a high shrieking sound by MMH] ... Yes, yes! Like at sports, but not fun, not funny, not loving not happy not ... not human.

Alexandar bent me all the way back, I was almost on the ground. I was frightened. Do you understand that? I was frightened. I didn't know what to do, I was upside down in a brawl that was not a brawl, it was a ... it was a ceremony, it was organized and broken at the same time, evil and careless all at once, strong against weak, big against little ... and they loved it, all of them, loved it. I could see faces passing in front of me, fast, red faces, and smiles, teeth, eyes full of light ...

I don't know how that is possible. One blood type on the grass? Only Alexandar's blood. No, no, you have to look harder, there was blood ... flying, rain ... You saw the blood on my clothes. No, no, no, it can't be only Alexandar's, it can't be. There was a man standing over me licking the blood off his lips and he was almost on top of me and his mouth was full of blood ... You have to believe me! I'm not ...

[Tape is paused here, Inspectors call for a break, 47 minutes pass on time stamp.]

I killed him with a pen. Yes, I agree. A bit dull of me, wasn't it? No ancient curled dagger, no sharp rock, not even a kitchen knife. A simple pen. From the EuroShop. Package of three, price one euro. I'm not in the habit of walking around with weapons. Where are the police when you really need them, huh?

Alexandar was underneath me, the rest of the men were hitting and kicking and I think biting each other, all around me. The weird thing was, nobody screamed. I could hear a kick landing or a punch breaking a nose, but no grunts, no cries, no swearing. My head was pounding, all that blood, from being half upside down. I could feel Alexandar breathing underneath me, breathing fast, like he was … well, coming. Did you find semen in his pants? Why can't you tell me that? He was my lover. Fine.

I lost my sense of self, self and other, apartness. I was in the fight. Not with my body. In my mind. I was fighting, but I had no … no enemy. No, that's not right. Have you ever been in a crowd and the crowd is moving one way but you want to move another, and you just give up? I tried to get up, I tried to get away. I was scared but not scared, I was … It was bigger than fear for my own survival, it was fear like a wave, panic. Fear and forgetting. No, that's not it either. Okay, it was like this: I was part of the violence but I was not taking part in the violence, I was safe. I've been safe all my life. I didn't want to be safe anymore. And I saw my chance. A perfect moment. Nerves and bones and stink, the raw stink of anger that was pure, clean, emotionless anger. It's a lie to say I was protecting myself. I could barely see the other men around me, and Alexandar, he just, he just held me, held me tight. The problem was, I didn't understand the rules.

So. So. I put my hand in my breast pocket – yes, the left-side pocket, you know that because of the blood, because I put the pen back, it's a habit, keeping the pen – I put my hand in my breast pocket and I found my pen and I clicked it open and I reached behind me and I dug out Alexandar's eyes and then I wet myself and fainted.

Anything to add? I wish.

Psychiatric Report. Martin Murray Heather.
Dr. Horst Mann, Chief Assessment Inspector, Berlin Brandenberg, District 11.

The patient Martin Murray Heather (heretofore noted MMH) exhibits severe dissociative symptoms, primarily as related to violent acts he believes himself to have committed. After taking MMH to the grounds wherein he believes himself to have murdered one 'Alexandar' [note: no such person of that name matches any description of known people in the Berlin Police Domicile Registry], and showing MMH the site [note: the site described by MMH is a large, grass-filled pit but in reality is an overgrown cluster of mixed plants, mostly weeds and a large wild rose bush], MMH persists in the view that he committed an act of violence at this location. Simple confusion over place, a lapse of memory regarding location and time/date, cannot account for the intensity of MMH's persistent and aggressive insistence that the events to which he confessed occurred, in the exact area toward which he himself led myself and two resident practitioners. As is typical with such severe cases, MMH became extremely anxious when presented with factual evidence contrary to his statements.

Nevertheless, it is the assessment of this office that MMH is capable of violence, even lethal violence. The dissociation between his statements and tangible reality do not exclude the possibility that he has committed acts of violence in the past, either here in Berlin Brandenberg, or elsewhere, likely his native Canada.

Despite the break from reality described above, it is the assessment of this office that MMH's dissociative memories regarding a violent action are, in fact, the lesser concern. As we know nothing of MMH's history prior to entering Germany, we cannot guess what suppressed trauma may or may not have instigated this elaborate delusion, and it is our opinion that the violent acts detailed by MMH did not in fact occur, either in the immediate or distant past, at least not within the jurisdiction of this office. The concern of this office is MMH's elaborately constructed world view, one he persists in clinging to even when he presents uncertainty regarding the 'crimes' for which he first came to this office's attention. In short: whether or not MMH ever committed an act of murder or another violent action is of secondary concern, as no physical evidence can be found to corroborate his claims. However, his substrata reality, a reality determined by a complex and apparently wholly made-up [consultations with Drs. Ballard and Christov of the Humboldt Humanities Department of Teutonic Folklore proved fruitless, other than to establish that MMH's system of occult references, codes, and monster symbols are wholly of his own devising] is the primary safety concern for this office, whose ultimate duty is of course to protect the public. MMH cannot function in society if he continues to perceive the daily functioning of the world as little more than the mere after-effect of a perplexing range of spiritual and magical forces colliding and in constant competition. In short, MMH does not recognize the basic codes of any social contract. Instead, he perceives all exchanges as between entities with varying degrees of power, entities that determine the actions of the world around him. MMH appears to have no capacity for self-actualizing, only for reactive gestures as proscribed by his menagerie of gods, demigods, demons, magical animals, and magical devices. MMH is a profoundly lost man. It is the view of this office that at some point prior to MMH's arrival in Berlin, he constructed an alternative universe, one over-determined by a panopoly of deities and supernatural beings, and, from this vantage point, entered into a foreign and unfamiliar environment, namely Berlin and its immediate environs, and, in the attempt to match his already estranged world view to a doubly estranged actual environment, became disattached to reality. This disattachment, as it currently manifests, makes MMH a danger to himself and to others. Indeed, his 'confession' may be driven by a subconscious desire to alert others to his inability to proceed further in daily life. MMH is warning the authorities that he has become dangerous by constructing an imagined violent crime.

It is the strong recommendation of this office that MMH remain in care, in partial or complete isolation, with attendant medications (as prescribed by facility doctors) until his conscious and subconscious minds re-fuse. Isolation is prescribed not as a punitive gesture but as a curative – MMH will stop seeing his artificial reality in action only if he is deprived of cues, material for his fictions, so to speak.

B ut I did do it. Poor Dr. Horst, pecking for answers. Silly bugger.

At the end of a path, behind two dying tangles of ivy, is all the evidence of my crimes. Someday a house will be built there, or a new playground – or two horny kids will settle in to rut under the stars – under a cairn made with pebbles and two-cent coins … the pen, the cards, Alexandar's shoes (filled with salt, for safety), one eye, one broken eye.

My quiet and studious minders watch for signs that I am getting better. I hate to disappoint people.

My floor is cleaned once a week. I find things under the bed, crusts and fibres and such. A shard of a rock, no bigger than a mouse paw. Easy to hide.

The new paint is soft, milky under the drying skin. Poke a hole, push the surface all around the prick, collect the gummy latex. Roll the gum between my thumb and forefinger. Big ball, body. Small ball, head. A man. Dust for hair, threads for arms.

When my minders come, I hide my little men, all my little men, between my toes. They never check the soles of my feet.

I have enough little men for a circle now, a coven. Thirteen. Six would do, five is the correct formula, but time is mine to burn. Thirteen little ghosts to raise, thirteen devils.

Sometime soon, I'll be trusted with a spoon, a soup spoon, maybe a rounded fork (never a knife), a scoop to eat with, a concave tool. And then I'll start over.

To the circle, a silver bowl. Ladled in the silver, blood, my blood. In my blood, my piss. In my piss, my spit. Cover the cauldron with my hair. Counter-clockwise, pull off the effigy heads. Drink the cauldron dry, swallow the bodies. Raise the dead.

Editors' Note

RM Vaughan left behind the completed but unedited version of *Pervatory* at the time of his death. He had intended for it to be published.

Knowing that Richard always welcomed a thorough edit, the three of us – Coach House Books editor Alana Wilcox and Richard's literary executors, Jared Mitchell and Jeramy Dodds – worked with the manuscript to make it a more cohesive novel. We made some cuts to the text, reordered it somewhat, and tidied it up, but we decided not to add anything.

Pervatory then stands as Richard's last word. We have tried to make that word a compelling and coherent read while respecting Richard's voice and vision. We've enjoyed spending a bit more time with a dear friend, and we hope you do too.

Celebrated, tormented, icono-clastic, highly original, and deeply funny, **RM Vaughan** is remembered and cherished as a novelist, poet, filmmaker, social commentator, and visual arts critic. Apart from *Pervatory*, he was the author of two other novels, *Spells* and *A Quilted Heart*. As a poet he published four volumes: *A Selection of Dazzling Scarves, Ruined Stars, Troubled,* and *Invisible to Predators*. In addition, his poems have been featured in many anthologies in Canada and abroad.

As a social commentator he wrote *Bright Eyed: Insomnia and Its Cultures* and *Compared to Hitler: Selected Essays*, a gadfly's volume of complaints about his favourite preoccupations: contemporary art, Vancouver, and baby boomers.

He was also famed as a playwright, having created and mounted *Camera, Woman*, an imagining of the life of pioneering female film director Dorothy Arzner; a psychological tour-de-force, *The Monster Trilogy*; and an ominous play about suicide, *One Year After*.

RM Vaughan's enormous output places him in the forefront of Canadian arts. If there was a tragic dimension to Vaughan's life, it was that he was a writer who never truly knew how loved and respected he was. RM Vaughan died in 2020.

Typeset in Arno and hand-lettering by Fiona Smyth.

Printed at the Coach House on bpNichol Lane in Toronto, Ontario, on Zephyr Antique Laid paper, which was manufactured, acid-free, in Saint-Jérôme, Quebec, from second-growth forests. This book was printed with vegetable-based ink on a 1973 Heidelberg KORD offset litho press. Its pages were folded on a Baumfolder, gathered by hand, bound on a Sulby Auto-Minabinda, and trimmed on a Polar single-knife cutter.

Coach House is on the traditional territory of many nations, including the Mississaugas of the Credit, the Anishnabeg, the Chippewa, the Haudeno-saunee, and the Wendat peoples, and is now home to many diverse First Nations, Inuit, and Métis peoples. We acknowledge that Toronto is covered by Treaty 13 with the Mississaugas of the Credit. We are grateful to live and work on this land.

Edited by Alana Wilcox, Jared Mitchell, and Jeramy Dodds
Cover design by Fiona Smyth
Interior design by Crystal Sikma
Author photo by Jared Mitchell

Coach House Books
80 bpNichol Lane
Toronto ON M5S 3J4
Canada

mail@chbooks.com
www.chbooks.com